CW00409747

FEAST

OF THE

SWAMP GOBLIN

A HORROR 'B-BOOK' BY

LEWIS STONE

Copyright © 2020 by Lewis Saddington.
All rights reserved.

AUTHOR'S NOTE

First and foremost, let me take a moment to thank you for picking up this book. As a lifelong fan of horror in its many forms, I hope reading this satiates your appetite for all things macabre as much as writing it did mine. But, before you delve into the bloody, twisted, schlocky terror that awaits on the following pages, I thought it only right to explain to you, the reader, why I chose to write such a tale.

I have always been a writer. From H. P. Lovecraft to Stephen King, from Robert. E. Howard to George R. R. Martin, my love for fantasy and horror fiction has burnt within me for as long as I can remember - and so has my dream of becoming a published author.

As some of you may know (but probably not), I am currently writing a series known as The Lycanthrope Saga. I consider this my 'serious' work. It is a dark fantasy series in which I am attempting to create a rich, intricate, plot-driven story that I hope will one day be an effort I am known and remembered for. If you are interested in investing your time in a gritty, fantastical tale about werewolves in their most ferocious, powerful form, then I highly recommend that you give that series a try.

I published the first book of The Lycanthrope Saga, Birthing the Beast, in early 2019. It was then that I realised I had thrown myself in at deep end, discovering that this series would likely be five or six books long, each one more challenging than the last. As much as I adore writing The Lycanthrope Saga, it's bloody hard work - as fantasy often is. Creating an entire world means an insane amount of attention to detail, painstakingly checking every sentence for internal consistencies, and I know that quite a few years are required for me to tell this story as well as it deserves to be told.

That's where this book comes in.

In order to not let writing my 'serious' work drain me of every drop of my creative juices, I decided I needed a side project. Something simple and thrilling, not to be taken seriously, but something I am as passionate about as fantasy - good old-fashioned horror. I decided that, whenever I have time, whenever The Lycanthrope Saga is taking its toll, these books would serve as the perfect escape to recharge and allow myself to just have some damn good fun with my writing.

Having studied Film Production at university, and having been obsessed with horror movies since I was about seven years old, I know that horror can be used to tell powerful stories. It often takes us to places few other genres dare to go, and nothing is out of bounds... but there's also something to be admired about the simplicity that so often comes with this genre too.

There's nothing wrong with wanting to shut your brain off and just enjoy a piece of entertainment that doesn't ask too much of you. Monster movies, slasher flicks, splatter-fests...

these are the types of films you can just sit back and enjoy the rush of on a Friday or Saturday night. Popcorn movies, if you will.

The same can be said for such books.

And so I decided that, with my love for all things schlocky and horrific, I would write my own B-Movies in book format - Horror 'B-Books', if you will. Short tales about monsters, murderers, and mindless evil in as many wild and wacky forms as my strange brain can conceive, written down and offered to anyone else who enjoys the same kind of (mostly) senseless and gore-drenched escapism.

Again, I must repeat - these books are not to be taken all that seriously. If you're reading this expecting the next Pet Sematary or At The Mountains of Madness, then you should probably close this book now. But if gruesome encounters with dripping creatures, twisted slashers, and countless other forces of evil is what you're looking for - with no lack of grotesque deaths at the hands of ungodly abominations - then I dare say you've come to the right place.

ONE

"Fuck."

The soft, moist ground threatened to swallow Samuel Hunter's boot whole. He grunted, heaving his leg upwards, an unpleasant *schlop* following as mud lapped back into the earthen hole his foot momentarily left behind. His recoil was quick, but not quick enough to keep the sludgy muck from slipping over the tongue and rim of his boot. He cursed again, grimacing at the cringe-inducing sensation of cold, wet filth seeping into his cotton sock.

"You watch your damn mouth," Duke Hunter grumbled, turning and raising an arm in front of his eyes to keep the flashlight in his son's hand from blinding him. He watched as Sam struggled to keep the forest floor from gobbling up his lower limbs, and he shook his head. Standing there in his designer's coat with his brown, perfectly combed hair, Sam hardly looked like the kind of nineteen-year-old who would take much pleasure in hunting through the mountainous forests of

British Columbia after sundown with his father. Then again, Duke doubted that many members of the younger (and softer) generation succeeding his own would care much for such activities. After all, tracking and hunting took a great deal more effort than sitting in front of a fifty-inch flatscreen TV playing video games, a hobby which consumed an unhealthy amount of his son's time.

"I can't even see where I'm walking out here," Samuel complained, exasperated.

"That's what the light is for," Duke quipped back, pointing at the torch with the barrel of his rifle.

"Don't you think needing a torch is a pretty clear sign that these aren't hunting hours?"

"Sam the smartass, as usual." Duke shook his head again. "The sooner you learn to watch where you're walkin', the quicker we can be done out here."

"Dad," Sam whined. "It's freezing, and it's already dark. We aren't gonna catch anything out here now, and you know it. Please... can't we just head back?"

"Y'know your whinging won't get you home any quicker, dont' ya?"

"Asshole," Sam muttered, but Duke was no longer paying him any mind. His gaze had already returned to the unidentifiable tracks marring the soft earth, tracks he had been fumbling after for the better part of an hour through the summer night. The pair must have been four or five miles from their remote campsite by now, a campsite which would be difficult to find now that the sun had set. Fortunately, Duke was a man who knew how to navigate wild terrains no matter the time of day or night.

Sporting his camouflage overalls and his hunting cap,

holding his rifle ahead of him, Duke led the way deeper into the widespread, unwelcoming woodlands, the light of the torch Sam was holding guiding him. The tracks, long-toed and slender, almost reptilian in appearance, continued north, with each one separated from the next by unsettlingly long strides. Duke had never seen anything like them in all of his forty-eight years, and he was determined to find out what abnormal cretin they belonged to.

Then came the *crunch* from beneath his boot. Looking down, his suspicions that whatever he was following was no common predator were confirmed.

"Is that a *skull?*" Sam asked, shining the torch at the ground, his voice cracking as the question passed his lips.

"Keen eye you've got there," Duke replied. Sam couldn't tell whether his father was being sarcastic or not. "Looks like a grizzly skull."

"A *grizzly* skull?!" Sam spluttered, his voice no longer breaking but outright squeaking in an almost supersonic pitch. "What the hell's out here killing *grizzlys?!*"

Duke was wondering the same thing. Not only was the skull broken, but it had been entirely stripped of all substance. Whatever had killed the beast clearly had a hunger for flesh, and flesh alone. Then, squinting through the thick veil of darkness ahead, Duke saw that this was only the beginning of his disturbing discovery. Taking the torch from his son's hand, he shone it ahead, and the beam of light illuminated what lay beyond where he was standing.

At the bottom of a slope above which they stood, amidst the fir and pine trees, a great swamp stretched into the darkness. The ground was almost invisible to the naked eye, a result of the dense and swirling mist that covered the earth across the floor

9

of the swamp, but many mounds of mossy land protruded from mist like haunting, miniature islands across the hellish landscape. And, among the islands, one especially large mound stood in the centre of the swamp, twice as tall as any man, its face opening into a cave-like shelter.

The slope leading down was steep, but not so steep that one couldn't walk down it, which was exactly what Duke began doing as he handed the torch back to his son.

"What the fuck are you doing?" Sam gasped.

"I told you to watch your language," Duke snapped.

"Fuck my language! This is creepy as shit!"

"Well, you ain't wrong," Duke agreed, "but I ain't leaving this unexplored. You wait here, and keep that light pointing down there so I can see where I'm going. I don't fancy breaking a leg tonight."

"Dad-"

"I'll just be a few minutes."

"That's a few minutes too long! Please, can we at least wait until the sun comes up?"

"There ain't nothing in the dark that ain't in the light," Duke said, as though his words were the wisest anyone had ever spoken. "I've got my rifle, and that's enough to keep just about anythin' at bay. Now do as I say, and we'll head back as soon as I've checked this out."

Sam, realising that his protests would only lengthen their woodland expedition, held the torch out reluctantly and guided his father down the slope. Duke soon reached the bottom and, when his right foot passed through the ghostly mist, it squelched into soft earth beneath shallow water. When he brought his left foot forwards to join it, the mist reached up to his knees and a wetness worked its way into his boots.

"God damn bog, that's what this is," he said under his breath, and began delving deeper into the swamp towards the hill cave.

Crunch. Crunch. Crunch.

Duke Hunter recognised the sound of more bones breaking beneath his feet, but he chose not to say anything until he returned. He knew all too well how much Sam would panic with the knowledge that yet more dead creatures (or what was left of them) lay in this cold and isolated marshland, their remains scattered throughout the patches of watery muck. It was only when he came within ten feet or so of the hill in the middle of the sea of mist, the interior of the small cave finally becoming visible, that this hardened Canadian felt the bite of fear.

More bones lay on the fungus-ridden floor within the opening... and not only the bones of animals. A human skull, a ribcage, and a spine were amongst the pile, all of them almost entirely stripped of flesh. Worst of all was one bone in particular - it appeared to be a femur - which still had a chunk of muscle clinging to it. An unfinished meal, sickening to Duke but appetising to whatever lurked in this ungodly place... and it was fresh enough to have not yet begun to rot.

Turning from the cave to his son and gripping his trusty rifle with coarse hands, Duke's chest tightened when he saw that Samuel was no longer there. The torch lay on the ground at the height of the slope above the swamp, still shining down into the gaping pit.

"Sam?! Sam, where the hell are you?!"

Rushing back through the mist, his feet splashing in the grimy water, bones cracking beneath his boots with every other step, Duke reached the base of the slope and began to climb back up. He slipped more than once, his left hand becoming filthy as he pushed himself back to his feet, his right still tightly wrapped

11

around his gun, and he soon came back up to the forested land overlooking the bog. When he looked at the spot where his son had been standing, he felt his heart skip a beat and his blood turned cold.

Lying on the earth was his son's arm, the sleeve of Sam's designer's coat shredded along with the flesh of his shoulder, his hand still gripping the bloodied yellow torch.

Duke barely even had the chance to wonder what may have happened. He might have vomited, had he had time, but the abnormal, unrecognisable, territorial growl that erupted from the trees to the side of him ended the mere seconds Duke had to grieve for his son. Turning and aiming his rifle, he was able to fire a single shot at the repulsively slender silhouette before a slimy claw came tearing through the night.

A searing pain followed, and Duke's guttural cry of anguish echoed through the forest with the gunshot.

TWO

The minivan pulled up into the forested crevice on the side of the empty mountain road, coming to a halt in the dirt opening that served as a car park of sorts. It stopped in front of an old, weathered sign that read *Badger's Trail*, and had barely even ceased moving before the side door slid open.

A tall, blonde-haired, six-foot-three heathen, ruggedly handsome and muscular, stepped out onto the empty road. Moments later an equally attractive young woman, her long hair the same shade of blonde, clambered out of the vehicle and took in the Canadian wilderness beside her companion. Towering fir and pine trees stretched for uncountable miles and, even though it was still early August, the wind was mildly warm at best this far into the mountains and wooded terrains of British Columbia.

"It's about bloody time," Jacob Wright, the athletic student - more accurately, *ex*-student now, like all of his comrades - exclaimed in a broad accent which could only have stemmed from the one and only county of Yorkshire in Northern England. He put his hands in the front pocket of his grey hoodie and sighed with relief. "If I had t'stay cramped up in that tin can for another moment, I'd have jumped out o'the window."

"I know what you mean," Skye Peterson, the petite blonde bombshell sporting a bright blue coat next to him, replied with a country twang she had earned growing up in rural Gloucester. "I can't feel my arse."

"Let me help you with that," Jacob grinned, and Skye giggled as her handsy boyfriend reached an arm around her waist and squeezed.

"Save it for tonight, guys," came another voice with yet another accent. Lauren Golde, a tall and brunette young woman wearing a black jacket over a yellow flannel, adjusted her crimson beanie as she departed the minivan from the front passenger seat.

Unlike Jacob and Skye, the other three companions on the trip had all been born and raised in London, though Lauren hadn't met the two still inside the van until their university years. It was there, at the University of West London, that the group had studied Film Production together, finally graduating with their Bachelor's Degrees only the previous month - something they were now almost halfway across the world celebrating.

"If you two are going to start dry-humping," Lauren continued, "at least wait until we've set up camp so you can spare us the sight of it."

"Try sharing a flat with this guy for a whole year," Peter Devlin chimed in from the driver's seat, opening the minivan door and stepping out onto the road. He scratched his short brown stubble and zipped up his dark green coat as he laughed. "I can assure you, the sounds are even worse."

"Peter's just jealous he spent his uni years with his face buried in textbooks." Jacob turned to Skye with a mischievous grin. "I had mine buried in better things."

Skye giggled, standing on her toes and giving her boyfriend a kiss on the cheek.

After the four of them had enjoyed a moment of taking in their natural surroundings, Lauren walked around the minivan to the trunk and popped it open. Pulling out the first rucksack within her reach, she threw it at Jacob just in time for him to turn and see it come hurtling towards him. The bag hit him in the stomach, and he gasped as he wrapped his arms around it, winded.

"Come on then, lover boy," Lauren jibed. "You might as well start using that frame for something useful."

"This frame is useful for plenty," he winked, and Skye punched his arm playfully. Then he threw the rucksack over his shoulder and leaned into the minivan through the open side door. "You gettin' out anytime soon, four eyes?"

"Jacob," Lauren said sternly, handing him another bag containing one of the three tents. "Play nice."

"Oh, come on." Jacob rolled his eyes, taking the bag in his hand and passing it to Skye. "Harry Potter knows I'm just messin' about."

Aaron Shaw, a small and feeble fellow with circle-rimmed glasses in a red parka, ignored the jibe and continued reading his old, tattered copy of *The Slime Beast* by Guy N. Smith. Realising that the fifth member of the group was in no laughing mood, Jacob shrugged and led Skye towards Badger's Trail, heading into the forest.

"Whatever. I'm going t'see if I can find a nice piece of wood t'look at."

"You need your girlfriend for that?" Peter called after him.

"Maybe she'll find a nice piece of wood t'look at too!"

Peter laughed as Jacob's voice answered from the trees. Then he started helping Lauren pull out what bags and rucksacks remained, calling to his friend still sitting in the van as he did so. "Fancy giving us a hand, buddy?"

Aaron remained silent, continuing to read his first edition 1976 horror book and saying nothing. Peter and Lauren exchanged an unsurprised look, and Peter sighed aloud before stepping around to the open door at the side of the small white van. He climbed inside and sat next to his childhood friend.

"How's it going there-"

"I'm fine," Aaron replied bluntly, pushing his glasses back over his nose and keeping his eyes fixed on the chapter he was reading.

"You fancy lending a hand with the gear?" Peter smiled. "The sooner we set off, the better."

Aaron remained straight-faced, closing the book and sliding it into his baggy parka pocket, hesitating before speaking. "I don't know why I came."

"Don't be like that, man," Peter said, nudging him cheerfully and trying to probe some enthusiasm out of him. "We're gonna have a great time."

"*You* are," Aaron said, his eyes finally meeting Peter's. "*They* are. I'm just the tag along. The fifth wheel."

"Excuse me," came Lauren's voice from behind the van. "You're the fifth nothing. There's only one couple here, and they're probably going to spend the entire weekend doing their own thing in their own tent anyway." She paused for a moment, then let out a sigh. "At least I *hope* they keep it in their own tent."

"See?" Peter smiled again hopefully. "I know you don't have much in common with Jacob or Skye, but there's nothing to keep the rest of us from having a good time. Besides, me and you go back way further than everyone else, don't we? We've been talking about travelling together for years. We're finally doing it, so let's make the most of it. What do you say, man?"

Peter wasn't sure how he expected Aaron to react. He did, of course, feel a little guilty. He and Aaron had been best friends since they had met in their first year of secondary school, and they had conceived the idea of a Canadian road trip long before Jacob, Skye, or Lauren were in the picture. Since the other three, friends they had made at university, had joined in on their plans, Aaron had been far less keen. He had even almost dropped out altogether, but Peter had made sure that that didn't happen.

Fortunately, after a short pause, Aaron cracked a smile. It was a little forced, but it was an improvement on the solemn silence he had been stewing in since they had landed in Vancouver three days ago. "You're right," he said, exhaling. "Let's just make the most of this."

"Good man," Peter grinned, and they climbed out of the van.

Gathering the rest of their backpacks and bags containing tents, food, and a rather hefty supply of various beers and liquor, the remaining trio left their rented minivan in the covered crevice by the road. Then, as they made their way up the rarely walked trail into the forest, they took their first steps towards what they expected to be a thrilling start to their travels. Little did this group of carefree twenty-one-year-olds know just how accurate their expectations would prove to be.

THREE

Despite its name, there wasn't a single badger to be seen on Badger's Trail. The gang plodded along with their backpacks, walking deeper and deeper into the forest, a forest which appeared even more vast under the cover of the woodland roof, where the height of the looming trees was even more astounding. The dirt path wound here and there, but it generally stayed at a slightly uphill slant, leading further and further from the road - and further and further from any signs of civilisation.

The males of the group marched ahead while the two young women lagged behind, each having their own separate conversations just out of earshot of one another.

"So does anyone actually know where we're going out here?" Aaron asked, adjusting his glasses and observing their natural surroundings.

"Not really," Peter chuckled. "I found this trail online a few weeks back, but it seems like hardly anyone ever comes here. There are plenty of places much closer to Vancouver and the surrounding areas for hiking or camping. It's totally isolated, which is what we want, isn't it?"

"I guess so," Aaron agreed. "But... is there a campsite at least?"

"Nope." Jacob kept himself one step ahead of the rest, asserting himself as the leader of the group with his position. "If there was a campsite nearby, there'd be other campers too. The whole point of this is t'find somewhere nobody'll disturb us so we can drink and fuck ourselves t'death. Well, just drink for the two o'you."

"We're not all total animals, dude," Peter laughed.

"Alpha male is the term you're lookin' for," Jacob retorted, looking back with a silly grin that showed he was only half serious. "Which reminds me, Petey boy... you finally gonna lay the moves on Lauren this weekend?"

"Dude, keep your voice down!" Peter said urgently, peeking over his shoulder to make sure that Lauren hadn't heard. Luckily, she was still deep in conversation with Skye, paying little attention to them. Peter turned back. "... but maybe, yeah."

"Come on, man," Jacob said, exasperated. "You've been holdin' back for way too long."

"I know, I know," Peter agreed. "I'm just... waiting for the right moment."

"Well good luck to you mate," Aaron said supportively, putting a hand on Peter's shoulder. "I hope it works out for you."

"Thanks man." Peter smiled at Aaron, glad to see that his best friend was chirping up more with every minute that passed.

"Soppy bastards," Jacob jeered at them both, faking a dry heave before addressing Peter. "If you nail her, that's good enough for me."

Peter and Aaron laughed. It was hard to keep a straight face around their well-built friend, a friend who often proved himself to be not entirely unlike a Neanderthal - both in stature and in intellect.

"So, you and Jacob seem to be going well," Lauren said to Skye as they followed the boys, perhaps twenty-or-so feet behind. "You must have been together for nearly a year now."

"A year last month, actually." Skye sighed heavily, brushing a strand of straight blonde hair from in front of her face. "Jacob forgot."

"Oh..." Lauren didn't know what to say. "Maybe not as well as I thought then..."

"It was great at first," Syke said, "but we've been messing around since last July now, and he still doesn't seem ready to commit. It took me nearly six months just to get him to change his relationship status on Facebook. It's starting to feel like it's just sex."

"Yeah, I bet that gets old quick," Lauren laughed.

"Trust me, it actually does."

"Well I wouldn't know about any of that." Lauren shook her head. "It's been a while."

Skye smirked. "I think we both know someone who would be happy to change that."

"What do you..." It was only when Lauren saw Skye motioning her head towards the guys walking ahead that she clocked on to what was being implied. "You mean... Peter?" She whispered the name.

"Come on," Skye rolled her eyes in disbelief that Lauren seemed so clueless. It was usually Skye who was the ditsy one of the group. "Have you seen the way he looks at you?"

21

"I... I haven't." Lauren thought about it for a moment. "Me and Peter have always been close since we met at uni, but just as friends. I don't know... that might be weird."

"Your loss," Skye shrugged. "I mean, he is pretty hot."

Allowing her eyes to linger on Peter for a few moments, Lauren couldn't help but agree. With his close-shaven and groomed beard, his styled hair, and his warm smile, he certainly had a face few girls wouldn't enjoy looking at - or sitting on. Glancing down at his tight black jeans, staring at his buttocks as his legs carried him up the slightly slanted trail, she realised his face wasn't the only thing about him that was worth looking at either.

"Eh," Lauren said, a sound of agreement. "I could do worse."

The girls laughed, and the guys looked back, clueless about what was so funny.

A couple of hours passed, and it was only when Badger's Trail showed signs of circling back that the clan realised they had gone as far as they were going to go with the guidance of the path. The guys stopped and waited for the girls to catch up, Peter and Aaron catching their breath after the lengthy hike while Jacob hardly looked like he had taken a step.

"Pussies," he said disapprovingly, laughing as the other two panted before turning to the girls who were also struggling to keep up. "Well, I think it's safe t'say that following this trail is pointless by now."

"What do you mean?" Skye asked.

"The path has levelled out. It'll probably just take us back down t'the road if we go much further, and if we set up camp near here, we'll just have people walkin' by every five minutes."

"Jacob, have you seen *anyone* since we left the road?" Peter laughed, motioning his hands around the apparently empty forest. "Hell, we didn't see anyone *on* the road for the last half an hour of our drive, and we must be six or seven miles from our van at this point."

"I'm just saying, the last thing I want is some stranger sticking their head in my tent while I'm sticking my head in this one." Jacob pointed a thumb at Skye with all the subtlety of a 3000W jackhammer. "And it ain't the head on my shoulders I'm talking about."

"Gross," Lauren said bluntly.

"But if we walk too far from the trail, nobody will be able to find us," Skye pointed out.

"Yeah... that's kinda the point of what I just said." Jacob turned to Peter. "Y'can tell I'm not bangin' this one for her brains, right?"

Skye kicked Jacob in the shin. "What I mean is, what if we get lost or there's an emergency and there's nobody around to help us? Dick."

Jacob pulled a face at her, and Peter glanced at each of his friends. "Any suggestions?"

"How hard can it be to find a good camping spot in the forest?" Aaron asked, raising an eyebrow. "All we need to do is find somewhere flat and away from the trail."

"The ground is pretty uneven here though," Lauren pointed out. "It might take some time to find somewhere we can set up three tents comfortably."

Jacob looked beyond the curving trail and pointed forwards. "You three head in that direction." Then he turned and pointed to the left of the trail. "Me and Skye will go and have a look this way."

23

"Can we at least just find a place to set up camp before you start finding excuses to go and fuck somewhere?" Lauren groaned.

"To be fair," Aaron interjected, "if we *are* going to leave the trail, it's probably not a bad idea to split up. We'll find somewhere quicker that way."

"See," Jacob said, nodding at Aaron. "Specky gets it."

Aaron flashed Jacob an irritated look, not appreciating yet another dig directed at him, but Jacob didn't even notice.

"Okay, fine," Peter agreed, already setting off and making his way beyond the trail. "We'll head this way, Jacob and Skye can head in that direction, and we'll all meet back here."

"What are we looking for?" Skye called after him and the other two that followed.

"Maybe an opening with a flat bit of land or something," Peter called back. "Somewhere not so far from the trail that we get lost, but not so close that we get disturbed. See you both here again in, say, half an hour?"

"Better make it an hour," Jacob grinned, sliding an arm around Skye's waist.

"You wish," Skye retorted, but she giggled at the feel of his groping hand nonetheless. Then, separating into two parties, the youngsters began their search for a decent spot to settle down and party in the wilderness for the weekend.

FOUR

After fifteen minutes of walking, Peter, Lauren, and Aaron found themselves completely removed from the trail and surrounded by unmarred nature. The late summer sun broke through the forest roof, shining down in orange beams that reached the earth, but it was noticeably cooler in the shelter of the woodlands than on the open road. Looking back to see how far they had come and realising that they hadn't stopped walking since setting off, Aaron paused for a moment. "Maybe we shouldn't wander too far from the trail."

"You're the one who sided with Jacob and suggested that we split up," Lauren reminded him.

"That was just to shut him up," Aaron clarified. "We all know he won't back down once he's made a point, even if nobody agrees with him."

"Let's just go a little further," Peter said, pushing on. "It doesn't matter how we find a place to camp, as long as we do it sooner rather than later. I just wanna crack a beer open around a campfire and have a good time."

"I don't think it really matters where we set up, as long as the ground is even," Lauren said, clearly fed up of walking by now. "Like you said, we haven't even seen a single other person since we got here. I doubt anyone's going to just pop up out of nowhere and-"

Turning around, Lauren couldn't help but let out a sudden scream as she crossed paths with a man walking directly ahead of her, bumping into him. Taking a moment to regain her senses, she broke out into a weak laugh and placed her hand over her chest. "Jesus Christ," she said shakily. "You scared the living shit out of me."

"Sorry darling," said the man. He was perhaps in his mid-twenties, sporting an open leather jacket over a Cannibal Corpse t-shirt. He ran a hand through his slicked-back hair and smiled, the impressive moustache on his upper lip curling as he did so. "Guess I wasn't looking where I was going, ey. I'm Ashley. This is Scott."

Ashley motioned his hand behind him to the bushy-bearded and messy-haired companion none of the group had noticed until now. Scott nodded, keeping his hands in his pockets and offering half a smile.

"I'm Peter," Peter said, stepping forwards cheerfully and shaking Ashley's hand. He turned to Scott, who pulled his hand out of his pocket and completed the handshake quickly and firmly. "This is Lauren and Aaron."

"Nice to meet you guys," Ashley said with a strong Canadian twang. "Didn't mean to scare you. We're just out looking for our dog, ey. He took off in this direction a few miles back. We heard you three coming, so I decided to head over and ask if any of you had seen him."

"No, sorry man," Peter told him. "We haven't been here too long. We're just looking for a place to set up camp. Didn't really expect to bump into anyone out here."

"Grizzly's Walk ends about three miles that way," Ashley said, pointing east. "We usually stray from the path and take in the country, but not this much. Got our pooch to blame for that, ey. What are you guys doing out here?"

"Travelling," Lauren cut in. "We just graduated last month. We decided we'd celebrate by getting away from rainy old England and taking a road trip across Canada."

"Oh, nice," Ashley said approvingly. "Well, if you walk about another twenty minutes that way, there are some pretty sweet spots where the ground evens out, ey." He pointed further in the direction the trio had already been heading.

"Awesome," Peter grinned. "Thanks for letting us know!"

"Don't mention it," Ashley said, then carried on through the forest with his quiet friend by his side.

"Do you have a phone number or something?" Lauren said, blurting out the question a little more enthusiastically than she meant to. She doubted that she would have chance to get in touch with this strikingly handsome stranger again before the group's travels continued, but getting his number wouldn't hurt too much if the suspicions about Peter's attraction towards her proved incorrect. A woman has needs, after all. She didn't see the way Peter hung his head in dismay, however, nor the way Aaron placed a hand on his friend's shoulder for comfort.

"I sure do," Ashley replied and, without saying anything, Lauren handed her phone over and watched as the leather-jacketed fellow entered his details into her phone before passing it back over. "Awesome. So if you see our dog, just let us know, ey? He's a big boy, a black Great Dane. Slobbery as hell. He's sure to come bounding over if he sees any of you."

"Oh, brilliant!" Lauren beamed. "I *love* Great Danes! What's his name?"

"Pickle," answered Scott, speaking for the first time.

"Pickle?" Aaron asked, unsure if he had heard properly.

"Yeah. Pickle."

Aaron and Peter exchanged a glance, but neither of them said anything. Scott didn't look like the kind of guy who would respond well to a jibe of any kind, even if his pet's name was practically begging to be poked fun at.

"Anyway, you guys enjoy your weekend," Ashley said, preparing to leave a second time. "Give me a call if you see anything! Maybe we'll catch you later, ey."

"Maybe you will," Lauren said, tilting her head and smilingly playfully. It was only when Scott took Ashley's hand that her smile disappeared.

Come on, babe," Scott said to Ashley, and the two male lovers walked off into the forest.

"Well..." Lauren exhaled, realising how misguided her embarrassing efforts to woo the handsome devil with the moustache had been. "That's disappointing."

She turned to see Peter, no longer looking dismayed at all, sniggering alongside Aaron at her expense. She flashed them a warning glare, and their sniggering immediately ceased before their search for the even ground they had been told about continued.

"Damn," Jacob said, proudly zipping up his jeans and stretching triumphantly. "I've still got it."

"Not exactly the hour you promised," Skye replied, fastening her own skin-tight jeans as she stood to her feet, somewhat less enthused by the intimate session they had enjoyed on the forest floor. Twenty minutes of kissing and foreplay followed by barely five minutes of rushed animalistic mating (animalistic on Jacob's part, at least) had left her somewhat dissatisfied.

Jacob waved away the comment. "You weren't complainin' a moment ago."

"Whatever," Skye sighed. As long as her partner was proud of his own performance, apparently that was all that mattered. "I wonder if the others found a good spot to camp..."

"It's not like we spent much time looking for one ourselves, is it?" Jacob pointed out. "Then again, I always hit the spot."

"I swear the person who loves you most in the world is you."

"You spent the last hour lovin' me a fair bit."

"The last hour, my arse," Skye muttered, and the two picked up their backpacks before making their way back towards the edge of Badger's Trail.

Judging by the unimpressed looks on the faces of the other three when the couple returned, it was clear that they had been waiting by the path for quite some time. Lauren tapped an imaginary watch on her wrist and crossed her arms, but Jacob paid her no mind, not even acknowledging the delay his and Skye's sexual shenanigans had caused their friends.

"I guess I don't need to ask what you two were up to," Peter said, noticing Skye's dirty knees.

"Having a better time than you lot, that's for sure," Jacob retorted, still looking exceptionally pleased with his lacklustre lovemaking.

"Well we found a good place a couple of miles north of here," Aaron said.

"Oh, sweet." Jacob looked back in the direction he and Skye

had come from. "We didn't find anythin' back that way."

"I'm sure you found exactly what you were looking for, bud," Peter commented, winking at Jacob.

"Right, that's enough of that then," Skye cut in, growing tired of hearing the entire group openly and casually discuss her and her partner's intimate endeavours. "Let's find this spot of yours. My legs are hurting from all this walking."

"That's not all they're hurtin' from," Jacob chuckled, and Skye squeaked as her boyfriend leaned over and spanked her on the behind.

"Christ," Lauren groaned, looking physically nauseous. "If this is what we have to listen to all weekend, let's just get it over and done with."

And on that note, the five of them began making their way north, through the uninhabited greenery of British Columbia towards the spot the rugged-but-helpful gay couple had told them about. They all felt relieved to be almost done with searching for a place to set up base, and excited to finally get stuck into their supply of booze, weed, and deliciously nutritious canned campfire food, far removed from anyone or anything that might threaten to interrupt their mischief.

If only they had known what awaited them, they would have turned around and made for the nearest town in their vicinity, never to go back into the woods again...

FIVE

The forest evened out before long, and a few small openings came into view. After choosing one particularly cosy-looking spot with just the right amount of room, the group began unpacking their tents and setting up camp beneath the orange glow of the setting sun. Jacob finished putting his and Skye's tent up in no time, and Lauren's was only a small pop-up tent for a single person, but Peter and Aaron were still struggling with theirs an hour after they had begun. Wrestling with the rods as he tried to slide them into the fabric, Peter cursed at his lack of success.

"Need a hand there?" Lauren asked.

"We've got it," Peter replied, clearly not wanting to appear incapable in front of his crush, though the messy and incomplete structure standing between himself and Aaron implied otherwise. Lauren shrugged and turned away, leaning over her rucksack and unfastening the sleeping bag which was attached to it. As she bent over, Peter couldn't help but stare at the sight of her perfectly round behind, and his attempts to stabilise the tent momentarily ceased.

"Peter," Aaron said, trying to get his friend's attention as he continued to struggle with the slender rods. "Peter!"

Snapping his head towards Aaron, Peter's mouth was still hanging open. "Huh?"

"The tent?"

"Oh yeah... sure."

Aaron laughed, and they carried on with their efforts.

Jacob was in the middle of rolling a joint so large that it resembled a parking cone, his head resting on Skye's thighs while she sat patiently on a blanket on the ground and watched, eagerly awaiting its completion. The gang had been especially excited about enhancing their experience of the wilderness in a country where marijuana was legal, and they had bought more than enough to last them the weekend from a dispensary in the city.

Jacob licked the paper, finished rolling, and held the joint up in front of his face. "Y'know what? I think this might just be my masterpiece."

He pulled out a lighter and prepared to spark the joint before Lauren interrupted. "Hey, Bob Marley. How about you and Skye help me gather some firewood before we knock ourselves out? It'll be getting dark soon."

Jacob rolled his eyes, but he placed the joint and the lighter in the baggy pocket on the front of his grey hoodie and stood to his feet. Holding out his hand, he helped Skye to her feet too. "Whatever you say, boss."

"We'll be back soon," Lauren told Peter and Aaron as she threw her sleeping bag inside her tent. Peter replied with a mumbled curse as he fiddled with an uncooperative rod, and

Lauren giggled. Heading into the surrounding trees, she and the two lovers began their search of the forest ground for a supply of firewood.

By the time the sun had set, and the glowing moon was rising in the starry sky above, the five of them were finally sitting around a crackling fire with a pile of sticks and dead wood large enough to see them over for a few hours. They shared a joint, and, as Peter took the last few puffs between Lauren and Aaron, Jacob was getting started on passing around a six-pack of Canadian Molson beers from the other side of the fire.

Peter cracked one open and raised it high. "Here's to a weekend to remember."

"Fuck that soppy bollocks," Jacob muttered, raising his own beer. "Here's to a weekend of getting well and truly fucked up!"

"I'll drink to that." Aaron raised his beer, then took a swig.

"See, I knew you weren't so boring, four eyes."

Aaron just laughed off the insult. He was too stoned to let such a comment bother him by now.

"Who's up for a drinking game?" Peter suggested.

"Always," Jacob replied enthusiastically. "How about... Never Have I Ever?"

"Do we have to?" Skye objected. "I hate that game. I always end up smashed."

Jacob smirked. "That's because you've done everything, ya slut."

Skye slapped Jacob on the back of the head as he took a sip of his beer, and he spilled a little down his hoodie.

"So who's going first?" Aaron asked.

"Well, considering this is a game made for horny students," Lauren said, "I think it's only fitting that Jacob has the honour."

"Fair enough." Jacob thought for a second. "Never have I ever... lost my virginity on a football field at midnight."

Skye sighed. "I never should have told you about that," she said before taking a drink.

The game moved clockwise around the fire, and Lauren was next. "Never have I ever had sex in a toilet cubicle during graduation."

"Son of a bitch," Skye groaned, then took a second drink alongside Jacob.

Then came Peter's turn. "Never have I ever turned up to a lecture so hungover that I threw up over my lecturer's shoes."

"Oh for fuck's sake!" Skye groaned, drinking for the third time. This was not going to be her night.

The game went on for a little while. After forty-five minutes Skye was already three cans deep, Jacob was finishing his second, Peter and Lauren were both one can down, and Aaron had only taken a few gulps of his first.

"Maybe we should play a game that'll get us *all* drunk?" Lauren suggested.

"Hey," Jacob said, raising his hands defensively. "It's not my fault the nerd's so boring he's not even finished half a can."

"Yeah," Aaron began with a raised eyebrow. "Because drinking to 'never have I ever had three STIs in one year' is a real accomplishment."

"Gotta live a little," Jacob said casually.

"And actually," Peter cut in, "I've known Aaron most of my life, and he can drink me under the table. I don't know how he does it, but it's true. No word of a lie."

"I'll believe that when I see it," Jacob smirked.

"Wanna bet?" Aaron challenged.

"When did you grow a pair of balls?"

"Is that a no?"

Jacob thought for a moment. "Fuck it. One beer every ten minutes. First person to give up loses."

"You're on," Aaron agreed. He finished what remained of his can and picked up a second. He and Jacob raised their beverages in unison and began drinking.

"Hey, do you think those two found their dog okay?" Lauren asked, turning to Peter.

"What dog?" Skye queried, her voice slurring slightly.

"We bumped into two guys on a hike when we split up earlier today," Peter clarified. "They'd lost their dog, but I'm sure it turned up alright."

"I hope so." Lauren looked over her shoulder into the forest. "I don't want to wake up to a Great Dane trying to eat my face."

"I thought you said you loved Great Danes?" Peter laughed, knowing all too well that she had only said such a thing to impress the moustached hiker. "Lauren, if one dog called Pickle is the most dangerous thing in this forest, then we really don't have anything to worry about do we?"

Before Lauren could reply, Jacob spluttered. He was drinking his beer too fast in an attempt to keep up with Aaron. Aaron smiled as he finished his can and prepared to move on to another. A faint but certain panic flashed across Jacob's eyes, and Lauren chuckled, forgetting all about the huge, missing dog that might be lurking nearby. Her worries about the risk of getting her face eaten disappeared and she continued enjoying her night, oblivious to how real such a threat really was - and not by the jaws of any Great Dane.

SIX

Ashley continued trudging through the forest with Scott close behind, struggling to see in the dark. Luckily, they had kept small hand torches in their pockets in case they stayed out past sunset - they often got carried away on their romantic hikes together - and they were heading back the way they had come, nearing Grizzly's Walk. They had given up the search for the day, deciding to make way for their car and endure the long drive back to Vancouver before returning the next morning, but Ashley was still calling their dog's name anxiously.

"Pickle!" he shouted, his voice shaky and distressed. "Pickle, where are you boy?!"

"We'll find him, babe," Scott said, squeezing his boyfriend's hand supportively. "He'll manage one night out here on his own, I'm sure. We'll come back at first light and we won't go home again without him."

Ashley nodded, shivering. It wasn't freezing, but it was cold enough that his leather jacket and his Cannibal Corpse t-shirt weren't enough to keep him warm. "What if something's happened to him though, ey? What if he came across a grizzly or... or something?"

"Don't worry," Scott smiled behind his bushy beard. "There's nothing in these woods tougher than our Pickle, ey!"

Ashley remained stressed, but Scott felt his partner's grip relax a little where it had been almost crushing his hand. "I guess you're right. I just hope that-"

Ashley was cut off by a deep growl. He stopped speaking and looked around hopefully. "Did you hear that?"

"Oh, I heard that..." Scott replied, shining his torch around the dark trees uneasily.

"Maybe it was Pickle," Ashley suggested hopefully. "Maybe he's nearby, or-"

Another growl came from the shadows to their left, not close enough to identify the source but plenty near to recognise that it was no animal either of the two men had heard before. A shiver crawled up Scott's spine. He took a step back, holding his torch out in front of him but failing to see anything other than towering pine and fir trees. "That didn't sound like Pickle to me..."

Ashley was less sceptical. Any hope of finding his precious Pickle overcame whatever common sense he had, and he raced in the direction of the growl. Scott considered going after him, but he hesitated at the idea of approaching whatever strange creature was snarling at them from just out of sight.

"Pickle!" Ashley continued to shout. "Pickle, come here boy!"

"Ashley!" Scott called after his partner. "Don't go running off like that! We need to stick together..."

Thud!

Ashley struck something and stumbled backwards. At first he thought it was a tree, but when he raised his hand to his face, he found that it was wet with a slime-like substance. Confused and dazed, he raised his torch... and before he had chance to comprehend the horror he was faced with, a hideous claw came down and slashed with inhuman strength.

Scott felt part of his soul die at the sight of his dearly beloved spinning around to face him... with no throat. The entirety of Ashley's neck, from the base of his chin to the top of his sternum, had been torn away, and blood poured profusely from the mortal wound. Ashley frantically clasped his freshly opened oesophagus, but red only kept on gushing between his fingers as he fell to his knees. He opened his lips in a futile attempt to breath, and his mouth became a miniature fountain of overflowing blood as his dying gargles faded. A final look of mindless terror lingered in his eyes, and then he slumped to the floor, his face landing in the dirt.

Scott didn't even raise his torch to the unnaturally tall and slender figure, a figure that waited menacingly behind the fresh corpse of his partner of three years. He turned and ran, fear overcoming his heartbreak as his mind tried to cling to some semblance of sanity. His legs carried him as fast as they possibly could and he fled into the darkness of the forest, though his panicked running was clumsy and uncoordinated.

Tripping, Scott fell forwards onto the ground, dropping his torch as he did so. Scrambling back to his feet, still refusing to so much as glance at what may have been pursuing him, he didn't even spare a second to retrieve the torch. He simply ran until he could run no more and his lungs screamed at him for a moment of rest.

"Fuck, fuck, fuck..."

Leaning against a tree trunk, Scott finally observed his surroundings the best he could in the dim light of the pale moon. He could make out nothing save for the outlines of the forest and, as he began to believe that he might be safe, his sorrow counteracted his fright. The image of Ashley choking on his own blood, the life leaving his eyes as they pleaded for help, was almost enough to make him scream in emotional anguish. The only reason he bit his tongue was his fear of meeting the same fate...

Then a gargling growl came from beside him, and his final coherent thought was the realisation that it made no matter if he screamed or not.

Scott shrieked with what breath remained in his lungs as he turned and saw a monstrous shape lurch towards him. An indescribable agony followed when a long-fingered, sharp-nailed claw forced its way into his chest, shattering his ribs and closing around his rapidly beating heart. In that final, nightmarish moment of life, the sweet relief of death was the only mercy he dared to hope for.

SEVEN

"Did anyone hear that?" Lauren asked, turning her head and looking into the impenetrable blackness of the mountainous woodlands. The darkest corners of her mind told her that it was a scream, but she quickly pushed such thoughts aside and decided that it was some kind of animal instead.

"Hear what?" Peter asked, cradling his beer.

"I thought I..." looking around and seeing that nobody else had heard the sound, she shrugged it off. "Never mind."

From the other side of the fire where he was sitting with Skye, Jacob spluttered on his beer. It ran down his chin, and he wiped his mouth with his sleeve before breaking out into a coughing fit. "Jesus... *cough, cough*... Christ."

"You struggling there, buddy?" Peter asked, finding amusement in Jacob's reluctance to accept that he had met his drinking match in a foe as unlikely as Aaron. His ego must have been suffering more than words could express.

"Just... *cough*... just give me a minute."

"You don't have a minute," Perter pointed out, looking down at his phone in his hand. "According to the countdown I have here, you have... twenty-three seconds to finish that beer, or Aaron wins."

"Alright, alright!" Jacob spat, bringing his Canadian Molson back to his lips and drinking, clearly in pain as he did so. He held his throat with his other hand and gulped with as much vigour as he could possibly muster, but he couldn't stomach what remained of his beer. He coughed and spluttered again, shaking his head, unable to carry on but unprepared to accept defeat either.

"Ten... nine... eight..." Peter counted down.

Jacob tried one more time. He took a single swig and almost choked, then threw the can aside angrily.

Peter grabbed hold of Aaron's hand and raised it high into the air. "We have our champion!"

The girls clapped and cheered, both of them relishing seeing Jacob finally be the one to get knocked down a peg. Jacob grunted and stood up, taking Skye's hand and bringing her to her feet. "Yeah, whatever. Come on babe."

The couple began making their way beyond the campfire, both equally drunk and stumbling. "Where are you two going?" Lauren asked.

"I need t'bury the shame of losing a drinking game to the king of geeks over here. What better way t'do that than by burying somethin' in her?" Jacob nodded at Skye, who wasn't really paying much attention.

"You're a lucky lady, Skye," Lauren said with a shake of her head. "Just don't go too far, either of you. We don't want to have to come looking for your drunk asses in the middle of the night."

"Yeah, yeah!" Jacob called from the forest. He and Skye were already speeding off for yet another round of outdoor forest frolicking.

Sanding up and stretching, holding out his hands briefly to warm them over the fire, Peter enjoyed the calm now that the most rambunctious member of their group had left them with a little peace and quiet. An insect chirped in the background, the only noise aside from the faint wind, and he turned to Aaron and Lauren. "Either of you fancy another beer?"

Aaron burped. After five beers down in less than an hour, he had certainly had enough, and he didn't want to burn through their supply on the first night. "I'm... *belch*... I'm good thanks."

"I'll have one," Lauren said, raising a hand. Peter nodded happily and disappeared inside his and best friend's tent to retrieve the booze.

Lauren turned to Aaron. "You really know how to drink."

"A nerd like me has to be able to impress the ladies somehow, right?" Aaron chuckled.

"You mean like Skye?"

Aaron's laughter stopped instantly. "I... I don't know what you..."

"It's okay," Lauren winked. "Your secret's safe with me. For what it's worth, I think you're in with a shot."

"B-b-but..." Aaron stammered, blushing. "What... what about Jacob?"

"Oh, come on," Lauren said, smirking. "We all love Jacob for who he is, but he hardly knows how to get a girl head over heels. His talents lie with getting their heels over their head instead. He and Skye are just fuck buddies more than anything else, and that never lasts."

Lauren smiled at Aaron reassuringly, and he forced a smile back. He had never been a lady's man, and he had grown used to believing that he never had a chance with any women he found attractive - especially not a beautiful blonde like Skye, who he could never seem to stop thinking about. Before he could reply, however, Peter re-emerged from the tent. In his hand, he held a bottle of Crown Royal whisky. "So how about that drink?"

"That doesn't look like beer," Lauren replied, her eyes widening at the bottle glistening in the light of the campfire.

"I had to keep some of the good stuff hidden from the other two, or there'd be nothing left by morning." Peter glanced at Aaron who, despite his drinking skills, was looking glassy-eyed and wavy. "On second thoughts, this guy might be more of a risk than anyone else."

Aaron only smiled dopily, and Lauren hesitated before remembering that the whole point of isolating themselves was to get wild in the wilderness without any disturbances. "Fuck it, why not," she grinned, and Peter opened the bottle.

Skye stumbled down onto the forest floor, giggling as she did so, and Jacob fell over her. He stuck his tongue into her mouth and she returned the gesture, kissing her apish boyfriend sloppily in the darkness. She fumbled for his belt buckle and unfastened it, and Jacob began moving down, kissing her neck and biting playfully. At first it was only tender nibbles, but soon his teeth grew careless. "Ouch!" Skye said, wincing. "Don't be so rough..."

"I can't promise anything," Jacob replied, his lips caressing her collar bone. Nonetheless, he slowed down and continued with a little less aggression.

"Ah, shit!" Skye hissed in discomfort, and Jacob quickly pulled his mouth away.

"I didn't even do anything that time..."

"There's something digging into my back," Skye said, pulling herself out from under Jacob and trying to roll over.

Skye arched her back and fumbled around on the ground beneath her before pulling out a small, metallic object hanging from what felt like a leather strap. She couldn't see it under what weak beams of light the distant moon offered through the treetops. Squinting, she pulled her phone out of her pocket and shined the light of the screen on the object. A black collar with a silver dog tag hung before her eyes, the leather snapped and the metal stained with what appeared to be blood. On the tag, a name was engraved.

Pickle.

"What's that?" Jacob asked.

"I... I think it's a dog collar," Skye said, remembering the discussion the others had had back around the campfire. "Didn't Peter say something about two hikers who were looking for their dog?"

"I'm not thinking about that right now," Jacob replied, his mind already wandering back to Skye as he fumbled to unzip her blue coat, grasping at what lay beneath.

"Is... is that blood?" Skye observed, paying her boyfriend no attention.

Sighing impatiently, Jacob rose to his knees and looked down at her. "Christ on a bike, are we gonna do this or not?"

Lowering her phone and looking up at Jacob, finally pulling her gaze away from the dog tag, Skye huffed. "Can you please, for once, just think about something other than what's between your legs?"

"I am," Jacob jeered. "I'm thinking about what's between *your* legs."

Skye scoffed and pulled herself away from Jacob, recoiling. "You're a pig."

Standing to her feet and brushing the dirt from her jeans, she zipped her coat back up and began walking away, leaving Jacob on the ground with his belt undone. Tucking his awakened and insatiable manhood away, he groaned aloud in exasperation.

"Where are you going?"

"To show this to the others," Skye said, not even turning around as she stormed off.

"What am I supposed to do?"

Angry but unsurprised that Jacob *still* wasn't paying any attention to the worrisome discovery of a bloodied dog tag, clearly only thinking about one thing and one thing only, Skye shouted back at him. "Stay here for all I care!"

And then she was gone.

Sitting on the earth, Jacob shook his head and ran a hand through his blonde hair. "Women," he mumbled, fastening his belt.

Peter and Lauren were sharing the bottle of whisky, taking their time and enjoying the warmth of it flowing through their bodies as they sat beside the fire. Stealing a glance at the stunning girl beside him every time she looked away, Peter felt his heart begin to race. He wanted to kiss her so badly, but the anticipation of waiting so long had built it up into what seemed like an impossible task.

Just do it, you idiot. Just do it.

Aaron was paying no attention to either of them. He was back to reading *The Slime Beast*, his face pale as he struggled not to vomit. He may have been able to handle his drink better than most, but drinking so much so quickly after not touching alcohol in a while was wreaking havoc with his stomach.

Lauren turned to Peter, and their eyes met. She took a swig of the whisky, her eyes remaining on his as she did so, her lips curling around the rim of the bottle. She swallowed, and instead of giving the whisky back to Peter, she placed it on the ground between them. Then she flicked a curl of brunette hair aside, and he was certain that he saw her quickly glance at his lips.

This is your chance, you idiot, just do it. Aaron's not looking, the setting is romantic, just do it man, just do it, just do it...

Peter finally plucked up the courage, and began to lean it.

Blurghhhh!

Lauren turned her head and watched as Aaron threw up all over the horror book in his hands. "Oh shit..."

"You alright there buddy?" Peter sighed, doing a poor job of masking his disappointment at the wasted opportunity.

"I... I'm good..." Aaron wiped his lips with his red coat sleeve. "I... I..." He jumped to his feet, raced over to the nearest tree, and continued to vomit into the dirt.

"Bless him," Lauren chuckled.

"We all have our limits," Peter replied with a half-smile.

"He did a better job than I thought he would," Lauren admitted. "I think the highlight of my weekend so far was seeing the look on Jacob's face when he got beat at his own game."

"Yeah, that was pretty special."

Lauren nodded in agreement, then picked up the bottle. "Another drink?"

"No, I'm good," Peter said, waving it away.

"I thought you wanted to spend the weekend getting hammered?"

"I do," Peter told her. "I'm just the kind of guy who likes to take his time with things."

"Oh really?" Lauren said flirtatiously. "Like what?"

Peter's heart began to race again, but before he could respond to the clear sign that now was a better time than any to make a move, Skye burst onto the scene. Thwarted once again.

"Hey guys," Skye said, still stewing over her boyfriend's lack of class.

"Hey Skye," Lauren replied. "Where's Jacob?"

Skye shrugged. "Being an asshole somewhere."

Lauren rolled her eyes. "No surprise there."

"What's that you have in your hand?" Peter asked.

"Oh, this..." Skye lifted up the collar. "It's a dog tag. I think it belongs to that dog those guys you mentioned were looking for."

Skye tossed the dog tag and Lauren caught it, holding it forwards to get a better look in the light of the crackling fire. She saw the name, and the stains that looked suspiciously like blood, and gave Peter a look of worry. "That can't be good. Maybe Jacob shouldn't be out there on his own..."

"You think?" Skye asked, suddenly feeling guilty about leaving her drunken and irresponsible boyfriend in the forest unaccompanied.

"I... I don't know," Peter cut in, not wanting to spoil the night with unnecessary concern. "It's probably nothing."

Lauren raised the dog tag, and when she spoke there was disbelief in her voice. "Did you even look at this?"

"There's bound to be some explanation," Peter continued. "Sitting here with an open fire, making all this noise... if there was anything worth worrying about out there, we'd have seen it by now... wouldn't we?"

The trio exchanged nervous glances as they dwelled silently on the question at hand. Then Aaron threw up again at the edge of the camp, and their attention was pulled away from the bloodied dog collar to the welfare of their drunken friend. Unfortunately, is was the welfare of their *other* drunken friend that was truly in peril, as they were all about to find out...

EIGHT

Jacob urinated against the body of a fir tree, grunting audibly as he relieved himself of the copious amounts of alcohol that had been swelling his bladder into a bloated balloon. As the beer left his system and steamed against the wood, he began to dread going back to the camp, knowing that he would have some making up to do. Skye often put up with his simple sexual ways, but, when she grew tired of it, he was forced to play the model boyfriend until she decided to warm up to him again. It was a charade he wasn't sure he had the willpower to go through, especially considering he didn't plan on remaining her 'boyfriend' upon returning to England anyway. The only reason he hadn't ended things yet was to avoid an awkward trip which had already been booked for months in advance. That, and the sex was great.

Snap.

"That you, Skye?" Jacob asked, finishing his business. There was no response. "Skye?"

Snap.

The sound of twigs breaking underfoot drew closer.

"Always comes crawling back," Jacob whispered to himself arrogantly, shaking himself free of the last few drops and tucking his impressive manhood away. He didn't have the energy for these games. He just wanted a weekend of booze, weed, and sexual satisfaction before they continued their road trip.

A presence loomed behind him, and, zipping up his jeans and fastening his belt buckle, he turned. "So I guess you couldn't resist coming back for a piece of this-"

Something swiped in front of him, as quick as a flash of lightning, and it took his body a moment to register what had happened. Looking down, feeling winded and out of breath by whatever had just lashed out, Jacob's mind struggled to acknowledge what he saw. At first he thought the night was playing tricks on him, but, when he held out his arms, his confusion quickly turned to terror.

He was holding his own entrails in his bare hands.

Dropping to his knees, the pain finally kicking in, Jacob began to cough up mouthfuls of blood as his intestines slipped out of the gaping hole in his stomach. They slid around between his fingers like uncooperative eels, refusing to go back inside his body, instead falling to the floor with a sickening *schlump.* He shook violently, his body going into shock at the extent of the harrowing wound, and he finally managed to wheeze out a few words. "Wh-wh-what th-the f-f-fuck..?"

He stole a glance upwards, tearing his eyes away from the savagely disfigured abs he had spent so many years in the gym trying to perfect. Something stood before him, almost humanoid in shape and stature, but thinner, taller, and much more crooked. Whatever it was, it stank like death.

Jacob's eyes caught the motion of something swiping down a second time, and he managed to let out a single cry before he was silenced forever.

Every head at the campsite turned as the sound echoed from the forest, and this time Lauren knew that it was a scream without any doubt. Peter looked at her, and his face went white. "Now that I heard..."

Straightening himself up against the tree he was leaning against, having finished his episode of vomiting, Aaron looked in the direction from which the deathly cry came. "Was that Jacob?"

Skye's jaw dropped and, covering her mouth with her hand in sheer dread, she began stumbling towards the forest. *"Jacob!"*

Lauren jumped up and caught her by the arm, almost dislocating her own shoulder when Skye tried to pull away. "Skye, we don't know what's out there!"

Skye yanked herself free from Lauren's grip and vanished into the trees, shrieking as she went. "We have to help Jacob!"

"Fuck!" Lauren cursed.

Immediately afterwards, Aaron also came barging past, pushing through his drunken state to pursue and protect his secret love. "We can't just let her go out there alone!"

"Double fuck!" Lauren cursed again. Just like that, she and Peter were left alone in the light of the campfire. She threw her hands in the air, exasperated. "Now what?!"

Peter looked around for a moment, searching for anything that could be used as a defensive weapon. His eyes settled on the flames and, leaning over, he seized a stick protruding from the fire and raised the burning end before his face. "Wait here. I'll go after them."

"Wait here alone?" Lauren spluttered. "Hell no. I'm coming with you!"

There was no time to argue. Leading the way with only his makeshift flaming torch for protection, Peter raced from the opening towards whatever horrors awaited them in the shadows of the forest, with Lauren at his heel.

"Jacob!" Skye screamed. "Jacob, where are you?!"

Even with a hefty supply of alcohol in her system, there was nothing that could numb the overwhelming panic Skye felt coursing through her. If any harm had come to Jacob, she would never be able to forgive herself. Why did she have to leave him like that? He was only being his usual brutish self. Sure, it grew tiresome and irritating at times, but she shouldn't have left him alone. She shouldn't-

Skye's train of thought trailed off when she saw something crouching up ahead. It was leaning over an inanimate lump, grunting as did so, crunching, squelching.... *eating*.

It was the mixture of fearful concern for her partner and morbid curiosity that pushed her onwards, closer and closer to the unusual shape moving in the black. She walked slowly, carefully, trying to keep her footsteps light. But, even with the utmost care, a young woman walking a forest floor littered with sticks and natural debris could not do so in complete silence - especially not to inhumanly sensitive ears accustomed to lurking and hunting in the darkness and the quiet...

Snap.

Skye froze. So did the figure. Then, her lower lip trembling, tears beginning to stream down her face, she saw what lay beneath the creature's grotesque, humanoid figure as it rose, and she could no longer silence her sobs.

Jacob was sprawled lifelessly between a pair of long, slimy legs, his stomach slashed open and emptied, his jaw torn off whole. His tongue, a tongue he had used countless time to taste and caress every inch of Skye's body, lay hanging out of his once-handsome and now-disfigured face, and his unseeing eyes retained a look of absolute terror. Some of his innards lay next to him, having spilled out messily, though much of the pile of steaming guts had already been consumed.

Then the looming figure came lurching towards Skye, and she closed her eyes in total resignation. She was utterly devoid of fight.

"Skye!" Aaron screamed, catching up and launching himself between her and the dripping humanoid. Had he seen its face, its hungry eyes, its open jaws, he might have regretted his decision immediately, but it moved too quickly for him to understand what he had just thrown himself before. A sharp pain sliced its way across his chest, and four deep gashes ripped through his zipped-up parka. Blood began to leak from the open wounds and, collapsing to the dirt, his glasses fell off and his poor sight became blurred. The monstrous form hung over him, stinking and foul as it moved in for the kill...

"Aaron!"

The sound of Peter's voice approaching was like music to Aaron's ears.

The creature snapped its oddly-shaped head away and, when the light of the fiery stick came into view, it screeched a devilish screech that threatened to perforate the eardrums of all those who heard it. Peter came to a halt, holding his flaming torch in front of his face protectively as Lauren clung to him from behind, and the murderous, flesh-eating monster could finally be seen by all.

Standing seven feet tall, its grey-green skin was scaly and fish-like, dripping glistening slime that seemed to ooze from a multitude of pores. Its limbs were long and slender, though there was something about the lean muscle beneath its tight skin that indicated an unfathomable degree of strength. And its face, almost too hideous to behold, consisted of pointed ears, a curling set of teeth that stretched to create the illusion of a sickening smile, and a wrinkled nose beneath a pair of eyes without pupil or iris - eyes of pure evil, reflecting nothing but an insatiable appetite for the taste of man.

"What the *fuck* is that..?" Lauren asked, and the oozing demon of the forest screeched again at the sound of her voice. "Peter, stay back!"

"It's scared of the fire!"

Peter bellowed the realisation as it came to him, and he lunged forwards with the flaming stick. The creature hissed hatefully, stepping back from the sparks and swiping for the stick with crooked fingers that ended with four-inch nails as sharp as razors. Peter pulled the stick back then lunged forwards again. Turning with a speed almost unfollowable by the human eye, the repulsive predator turned and retreated into the night, leaving the group to try and make sense of what they had just witnessed. The sound of its hateful shrieking faded, and Skye's grief-stricken sobs replaced it while she knelt over the still-warm corpse of her mangled and partially devoured partner.

Jacob was beyond help. Aaron, however, remained on the earth, bleeding heavily from the wounds he had sustained across the length of his chest. Peter raced to his best friend's side, using the burning torch to see and assess the injury. "Hang in there, buddy," he said, keeping a brave face on display despite his panic. "We need to get you to a hospital."

"The nearest hospital is over fifty miles away!" Lauren yelled. She stood at Skye's side, trying her hardest not to puke at the sight of Jacob's remains, and pulled out her phone. "There's no fucking signal to call for help here either! Christ... what *was* that thing?!"

"How would I know?!" Peter snapped back, throwing the almost burnt-out stick aside. "But Aaron needs help, and I'm not just going to sit here waiting for it to come back. So how about you get over here and give me a hand?"

Understanding that Skye would be a heartbroken wreck no matter what, Lauren reluctantly left her and walked over to Peter. She slid an arm under Aaron's right shoulder and, when Peter did the same with his left, they hauled him to his feet. Aaron moaned and lifted his head. "My... my glasses..."

"You'll have to forget about those for now, dude," Peter told him. "You aren't going anywhere on your own anytime soon anyway."

They began hobbling through the forest. At first Lauren tried to turn in the direction of the camp, but Peter stopped her. "I think the road is that way..." he said, realising that they had fled the camp in a direction leading even further away from their minivan.

"But what about..." Lauren 's voice trailed off. She didn't want to bring too much attention to the possibly fatal wounds Aaron was already perfectly aware of.

"Like I just said, he needs a hospital," Peter snapped. "We don't have anything to treat an injury like that, and the longer we wait, the worse it'll get. Our best bet is to try and make it to the minivan and hope that thing doesn't come back."

Lauren swallowed and nodded. Then, glancing back over her shoulder, she saw that Skye was still mourning by Jacob's mutilated body, something the rest of them had been too shocked to do up until that moment. Finally the reality hit that their dear friend, the humorous brute that had been Jacob Wright, was gone. All at once, the group fell into a grief-stricken silence, and their sadness matched their fear.

Lauren shifted Aaron's weight over to Peter and stepped back to Skye, dropping to her knees beside her. "Skye..."

"I... I can't leave him..." Skye wept, her hands covered in blood from clinging to Jacob's hoodie.

"We'll... we'll come back for him," Lauren said softly, her own voice breaking. She wrapped her arms around her friend. "I promise. But right now, we can't stay here. I need you to be strong. Can you do that for me?"

Skye wiped her nose, looked down at Jacob, then pulled her eyes away. Finally, she inclined her head in a pained nod, though it clearly took a great deal of mental effort. Lauren helped her to her feet, and, after a second heartfelt hug, she went back to supporting Aaron alongside Peter.

Lauren and Peter exchanged an uncertain glance. With one friend dead, another gravely wounded, and the third reduced to a blubbering mess, it was down to them to keep things together. With no time to adjust to the change in circumstances, no time to even try to process how their night had changed from the beginning of a fun weekend to a struggle for survival against an unidentifiable abomination, they began their lengthy and aimless walk in search of the road.

With every step they took, they could only pray that the demonic thing wouldn't return for a second helping.

NINE

"How're you feeling, buddy?" Peter asked as he and Lauren carried their friend through the woods. The bleeding from Aaron's four incisions was beginning to lessen, but his face had turned a ghastly white and his skin was growing cold.

"Like I've just had my chest slashed open," Aaron spat, forcing a laugh which turned into a pained cough. Peter smiled, but when he looked up at Lauren, the smile faded. Her expression was morbid, and she didn't need to speak to make her thoughts known - it was likely that Aaron wouldn't survive the walk to the road, and that was if they were even walking in the right direction. The black and uneven woodlands were almost unnavigable.

"Keep up, Skye," Lauren called back softly. Skye had been following like a zombie for the last half an hour, absent-minded since being forced to leave Jacob's body behind. Her hands were still red with blood, and she kept looking at them, each time with just as much horror as the last.

Realising that their efforts were unpromising at best, Lauren motioned towards a tree and began lowering Aaron against it carefully. "We'll wait here for a minute or two. Just to catch our breath."

Peter helped to carefully prop Aaron up against the trunk, and the two of them gave him some space as they scanned their surroundings. "I'm not sure this is the right way..." Lauren began, but Peter wasn't having any of it.

"It is," he replied, trying to make himself sound more certain than he actually was. "I'm sure it is."

"Peter..." Lauren said, touching his arm tenderly and taking him a few steps further away from Aaron and Skye, speaking in a hushed tone. "We can't go on like this."

"What do you mean?"

"We aren't going to make it."

"Well, what do you suggest?"

Peter was growing more agitated by the second, and for good reason. On top of Jacob's death, his best friend's life was also on the line, which was why Lauren dreaded what she was about to say. "Maybe we should split up..."

"Lauren!" Peter gasped. "We're not leaving anyone!"

"Keep your voice down!" Lauren shot back, but Peter only repeated himself.

"We're *not* leaving anyone."

Lauren thought for a moment while she tried to find the right words. "I don't mean it like that. But Aaron can barely walk, we're moving too slowly, and we might not even be heading in the right direction. With that thing still out there... Christ, that thing... we're sitting ducks. We all stand a better chance if we get help sooner rather than later. Even if just one of us goes ahead alone-"

"Wait," Peter cut her off. "Look."

Lauren turned and, when she looked where Peter was pointing, she saw what he had noticed in the distance. Headlights.

"It's the road," Peter said, his voice filled with hope.

"Oh, thank God," Aaron groaned.

Rushing back to their friend's side, Peter and Lauren pulled Aaron to his feet and began carrying him towards the road ahead, with Skye following only a few steps behind.

When the group emerged from the trees and onto the road, they were somewhat dismayed to find that it wasn't the main road they had taken through the mountains. Instead it was some rural dirt road, passing through the forest, with no signs indicating where it may lead to in either direction. But, despite it not being exactly what they had hoped for, nothing could wipe away the relief of seeing an old, rusty pick-up truck parked a few feet away, the headlights on and the engine running.

Skye took a step closer. "Th-this looks like th-the pick-up truck m-me and J-J-Jacob were in when w-we first had s-s-s-"

"That's nice," Peter said, interrupting her before she could finish her sentence. His thoughts weren't exactly on Skye and Jacob's past carnal relations at that moment. They were on the truck and its apparent lack of owner. "Where's the driver? There's nobody here."

"And what's all this?" Lauren said, analysing the bed of the truck. It was covered by a thick plastic sheet, but multiple large, strangely shaped items beneath formed lumps in the waterproof material. She gave all of Aaron's weight to Peter and stepped up to the rusty vehicle, tracing her hand over the sheet curiously. "Should I..?"

61

"Go ahead," Peter urged her on, and Lauren cast the sheet aside.

The bed of the truck was filled with an abundance of supplies, and not the kind one would expect to be used for hiking or camping. There were six red plastic canisters of flammable fuel, a rather hefty collection of metal beartraps, and a toolbox - all piled up in front of a long and lumpy object, wrapped tightly in a blanket and fastened with rope. It was then, upon closer scrutiny, that Lauren saw the bloodstains, and realised that the wrapped-up object was a body.

"Oh fuck-"

"Nobody move!"

Lauren froze. Standing in the truck's headlights, their face shadowed by a hunting cap, was a stocky man dressed entirely in camouflage gear, pointing a hunting rifle at the group of youngsters. None of them moved a muscle, and the figure edged slightly closer.

"Get away from the truck and put your hands in the air. *Now!"*

"Please," Lauren began. "Our friend..."

"I didn't ask you to talk, sweetheart," the armed figure snapped in a rough and gravelly Canadian accent. "Put your hands where I can see 'em! *Do it!"*

"I can't let go of him," Peter said as calmly as possible, not wanting to escalate the situation. "He's hurt."

The figure went quiet for a moment, then snarled and spat a glob mucus onto the dirt. "One bad move and I blow all of your fuckin' brains out, y'hear?"

"We just need help!" Lauren screamed, angry, impatient, and desperate. "Our friend needs a hospital. Someone is dead, and we-"

"Dead?" the rifle-wielding man asked, the first word he had spoken without shouting. He began to lower his gun. "How?"

"We were attacked," Lauren told him. "There was something in the woods. We-" She tried to step forwards, but the man raised his gun once more. She stopped dead in her tracks, attempting to make out the unwelcoming stranger's face, but she couldn't see anything beneath the shadow of his cap. "Who are you?"

At first, there was no answer. The man remained motionless, keeping his face hidden. Then, finally stepping forwards, he lifted his head.

His cheeks were wind-kissed and red, his jaw covered in a thick and greying beard. His mouth was frozen in a hateful frown, and he had dark bags beneath his eyes - beneath one eye, at least. The other was missing, covered by a white, blood-soaked bandage which did little to conceal the four parallel claw marks that marred the right side of his face, stretching over the socket from his ear to his forehead. Spitting, he lowered his rifle for good, and glared with his remaining eye.

"Someone you don't wanna fuck with."

Despite his hard exterior and challenging personality, the presence of this stranger - Duke, as he introduced himself - was a genuine stroke of luck. He immediately began seeing to Aaron's wounds, sitting him in the truck while he patched him up with bandages from a medical kit. He was hardly a doctor, but his work seemed like it would suffice in keeping their friend alive for the time being.

Finishing treating Aaron's chest, Duke noticed Lauren worriedly staring at the packaged corpse in the bed of the truck. "Do I really need to tell you that wasn't my doing?" he asked gruffly, and Lauren shook her head.

"You have to take us to a hospital," Skye demanded, speaking for the first time since Duke's appearance. "You have to help us get-"

"I don't have to do shit, blondie," Duke growled. "I've got bigger fish to fry."

"Can't you at least take us to the nearest town?" Lauren pleaded.

"Sorry kids." Duke shook his head. "I can't afford to waste another minute out here. What happened to your friend is gonna keep happening until someone does something about it. That fuckin' goblin, or whatever the fuck it is, needs takin' care of. You've already delayed me longer than I'm comfortable with."

"You're taking us to a hospital," Peter shot back, growing tired of this grizzled hunter's needless lack of cooperation. "This isn't a debate."

"No, it ain't," Duke agreed. "Seems to me you lot won't last another ten minutes out here on your own. I'm the biggest help you're gonna get tonight, so I suggest you show me a little fuckin' gratitude for fixin' up your pal and pipe the fuck down before you *really* piss me off."

"Gratitude?" Peter replied angrily. "You're leaving us to die out here!"

"I'm not doing shit to you. I'm just not leaving. Not until my job is done."

"What about your truck?" Lauren asked hopefully. "Can we take that at least?"

"Sorry," Duke said, taking his rifle from where he'd placed it on top of the roof of the truck whilst he had tended to Aaron's partially shredded torso. "Need it."

64

It was then that Peter clenched his fists, stepped forwards, and found himself being held at gunpoint for a second time that night.

"You got somethin' to say, boy?" Duke challenged him. "Those fists of yours are looking awfully tight. You gonna try somethin'?"

"Maybe I am," Peter retorted through clenched teeth.

"Think you stand a chance?"

"There are four of us."

"Three, unless you're counting mincemeat here," Duke corrected him, nodding at Aaron. "And I doubt the snivelling blonde could do much either, so that leaves you two." He waved his rifle at Peter and Lauren. "And I'd bet my left nut that I could gun both of you down before either of you even managed to lift a finger. So go ahead. Try somethin'."

Peter was seething, but, as Duke turned with a grunt and began sorting through what equipment he would or wouldn't be needing for his pursuit of the creature - the goblin, as he had called it - Lauren took her friend aside. "I'll handle this," she said quietly.

Knowing how often men felt the need to prove their dominance over one another through stubbornness and aggression, she chose a different approach - the approach of diplomacy. She came up beside Duke as he sifted through the truck bed.

"We really appreciate what you've done for us... for Aaron... so far. But is there *anything* we can do or say that might change your mind? We can't stay out here alone, and Aaron won't make it through the night."

"He might." Duke rummaged through his toolbox, gathering ammunition.

65

"How do you know?" Lauren asked doubtfully.

"Look at my face." Duke pointed at the bloodied bandage covering his missing eye and the ghastly claw marks. "I've been out here like this for three days. Do I look like someone who doesn't know all there is to know about survival, even under the shittiest of circumstances?"

"I guess not," Lauren receded.

"You guess right." Duke pulled his hand out of the toolbox, holding as many bullets as he could fit between his coarse fingers. "You guys got a camp nearby?"

"We have a few tents, maybe half an hour away. Why?"

"We'll head back there. If your friend rests up, he should make it until morning. And as much as you kids have been a pain in my ass so far, I imagine you wouldn't object to a little protection."

"Maybe not," Peter said, making his way back into the discussion, "but it sounds like a pretty stupid idea, sitting around a campfire and waiting for that thing to return, if you ask me."

"Good thing nobody asked you then, ain't it?" Duke grumbled. "That *thing* hates fire. It shouldn't get too close, not without me seeing it first."

"But it'll still know where we are!" Peter protested. "You'll end up bringing it straight to us!"

Duke said nothing at first. He reached into the chest pocket of his camouflage jacket with his spare hand, pulled out an open packet of cigarettes, and placed his lips around one of the protruding ends, removing it with his mouth. Tucking the cigarettes back away, he reached into another pocket by his hip and took out a small box of matches. Still gripping his rifle with his right hand, he used his left to shimmy a match out of the box before striking it with his thumbnail, lighting it smoothly.

Bringing the flame to the tip of the cigarette and inhaling, a cloud of smoke surrounding his face, he propped the rifle over his shoulder. When the smoke cleared, his lone eye became filled with one thing and one thing only - the desire for blood.

"That's exactly what I intend to do."

TEN

The campfire was, much to the luck of the group and their reluctant new companion, still burning slightly upon their return and thus easier to find in the dark. As they settled back down the best they could, Peter threw more wood onto the dying fire while Lauren and Skye helped Aaron into one of the tents. He was still pale, weak and barely able to stand from the blood loss, and he groaned in agony when they laid him down. "I'm going to stay with him," Skye said as Lauren departed the tent. "That thing would have killed me if it wasn't for him."

Lauren nodded and left Skye to keep Aaron company, joining Peter on a blanket by the growing flames as Duke finished surveying the surrounding wooded abyss of blackness. He had brought some of his supplies with him, with a helping hand from Peter - the medical kit, some beartraps, a single canister of fuel, and his rifle - and it was a good half an hour before his preparations ceased and he seated himself on the opposite side of the fire, lighting another cigarette.

"Got any beer?" he asked, his face lit up by the crackling flames, the light revealing the true grisliness of his facial wound as he cast his burning match into the fire and smoked. When his request wasn't instantly catered to, he took another drag on his cigarette and raised an eyebrow. "You're telling me you kids came out here to party without a drop of alcohol? I've been in these woods for three days. A beer is the least you can do for me."

Peter stood, reached into his rucksack which was lying nearby, and threw a can over. Duke caught it, tapped the lid, and cracked it open. It must have been warm by now, but he didn't mind, gulping greedily as the beer spilled down his greying beard.

"So... Duke..." Lauren began.

"Hunter." Duke wiped his beard with his sleeve, placing the can on the ground beside him. "The name's Duke Hunter."

Of course it is, Lauren thought. "What are you doing out here, anyway? Do you know what that thing is?"

"I don't think *anyone* knows what that thing is," Duke replied. "As I said before, looks like a goddamn goblin or something to me."

"Aren't goblins supposed to be small?"

"Not this one."

Peter sat back down next to Lauren and eyed Duke up and down, still sceptical of the man after their near-physical confrontation by the truck. "Why are you hunting it? This... *goblin...* or whatever?"

Duke stared at Peter with his one good eye for so long that it made the young man feel uncomfortable, but he eventually answered. When he did, his voice lost some of its gruffness, growing softer and almost unintimidating. Almost.

70

"Me and my son were hunting after sundown three days past. I didn't get to see him much... he lived with his mother out in the city... and I guess it was just my way of trying to bond with him. Maybe even make a man out of him. City life turns you young'uns soft. Anyway, we went a little too deep into the woods and... I guess we disturbed something we never should've disturbed. It was my fault. He kept telling me we should turn back, but I wouldn't listen, stubborn old bastard that I am." Duke took another drag, his one eye looking forlorn and saddened as it produced a single tear. "I should've listened."

"Is that... is that who you have in the back of your truck?" Lauren asked.

Duke nodded. "His name was Sam."

Suddenly, Peter felt guilty for the way he and the middle-aged hunter had gotten off on the wrong foot, even if that was more Duke's doing than his. "I'm sorry for snapping at you earlier, man," he said apologetically. "We were all just really riled up."

"Don't mention it," Duke shrugged, wiping the single tear away. He threw what was left of his cigarette aside, picked up the can of beer, and finished that too.

"How has that thing been out here all this time without anyone knowing?" Peter probed. "How has nobody else seen it yet?"

"I suspect they have," Duke answered. "Probably just that none of 'em lived to tell the tale. Not many folks come out this way though. I'm surprised you kids did. I guess that's what you call shit luck." He looked out into the forest thoughtfully, surveying the dark pine and fir trees. "I don't reckon it's from 'round here anyway, truth be told. No, seems to me it came from somewhere farther and even colder, though I couldn't tell

71

ya why. It likes the damp and the cold, y'see. Likes the dark too. It only hunts at night, as far as I can tell."

"And you think you can kill it?" Lauren asked hopefully.

"I *know* it. It bleeds just like everything else. It took my damn eye out first time I saw it, but I managed to fire a shot off into that sonuvabitch. Damn thing screeched so loud it nearly deafened me. It might be big and strong as hell, but it ain't immortal and it has its weak spots."

"Like what?" Peter asked.

"Fire, for one," Duke clarified.

"Yeah, we figured that one out," Lauren replied. "It ran away when Peter got close to it with a flaming stick earlier."

"Yeah," Duke grunted, scratching his bandaged facial scars. "Don't kid yourselves, though. You got lucky. It probably just wasn't expectin' a fight. Next time it will be..."

Screeeeeeeeeee!

The screech echoed from somewhere in the forest, almost as though the goblin was telling them... promising them... that, next time, it definitely *would* be ready for a fight.

"That was close," Peter gasped, jumping up. "Way way *way* too fucking close."

Duke, seizing his rifle from the ground beside him, lurched upwards. Raising it in front of his face, he began edging towards the rim of the circle of pulsating light created by the campfire.

"You're not going out there alone, are you?" Lauren asked Duke, standing and grabbing Peter's arm fearfully.

"I've survived out here alone so far," the hunter told Lauren confidently. "I think I'll manage."

For a moment, Peter forgot about the immediate danger of a flesh-eating goblin and felt a spark of joy as his crush grappled him for safety. Then Duke took a step into the darkness, and

Peter's thoughts returned to the threat at hand. It was the possibility of the gangly creature in the forest chowing down on him that he needed to be focused on, not Lauren - as much as he had fantasized about her chowing down on him in the past too, though not quite in the same manner.

And, just like that, Duke was gone. Peter and Lauren stood alone in the camp, huddling in the warmth of the flames and fearing the grotesque being that still lurked nearby, waiting for its chance to strike again.

ELEVEN

Skye tenderly ran her fingers through Aaron's hair as he shivered violently, huddled inside his sleeping bag. Beneath the fabric cocoon, he also had Skye's winter coat wrapped around him in addition to his parka in an attempt to keep warm. He had rejected the offer at first, not wanting her to get cold and trying to remain a gentleman despite feeling like he was knocking on death's door... but his mind had changed the moment she began unzipping her coat. Revealing a slim-fit black t-shirt, her breasts bulging at the v-neck, Aaron quickly quietened down and allowed her to remove whatever clothing she wanted to in her efforts to make him comfortable.

"Can I get you anything?" Skye asked, leaning close and placing a hand on his forehead to check his temperature.

"Erm..." Aaron hesitated, staring at her generous cleavage as her busty chest moved within inches of his face, her blonde hair tickling his cheeks. He only wished he still had his glasses so he could properly enjoy the view. "No... thank you... I'm good."

Skye nodded and leaned back. Then, once again, she began to cry. "I'm so sorry," she sobbed. "This is all my fault."

"You know that's not true," Aaron wheezed, wishing he wasn't in such terrible shape. He would have given anything to have been able to lean forwards and comfort her at that moment. "None of us could have avoided this."

"I know..." Skye whimpered. "But... I should never have run off like that. I should never have left... left Jacob..." her voice broke and she covered her mouth.

"I'm sorry about what happened," Aaron said. It was true. He may not have liked Jacob all that much, and Jacob may never have been kind to him, but he didn't deserve a death like that. Nobody did... and Skye certainly didn't deserve the trauma of seeing her partner reduced to a slender goblin's mangled meal.

"It was so stupid." Skye dried her eyes with her hands, fighting away the tears as best she could. "The last time we spoke before I left him, we... we were arguing. That's all I can think about."

"What were you arguing about?" Aaron asked softly.

Skye sighed. "Nothing really. We argued about the stupidest shit all the time."

"I thought you were happy with him," said Aaron. How could she *not* be happy with a tall, athletic, handsome man like Jacob?

"*He* was happy," Skye clarified. "He got everything *he* wanted."

"Like what?" Aaron asked. Skye flashed him a glance that said *really?* and Aaron understood that it was a stupid question. "Oh, yeah. Of course. *That.*"

"I mean, it was fun when it began," Skye continued. Now that she was finally spilling the beans about her failing relationship, it all came out at once. "You're *supposed* to just have sex and get fucked up every night at uni, right? But I just started to want more, and Jacob never seemed ready to commit to me. Not truly."

"Why not?!" Aaron blurted out, surprised that anyone could struggle to appreciate a girl as beautiful as the one before him. Then, realising how he had just lost his cool, he reeled his disbelief back in. "I mean... I just don't get why he found it so hard."

"I just don't think he'd ever taken a girl seriously in his life," Skye said, apparently still not noticing Aaron's blatant infatuation with her. "He could be a decent guy, but when it came to knowing how to keep a girl... not so much."

"I would take you seriously." The words came out unexpectedly and, for a moment, Aaron's mind quickly began to search for a way to backpedal. Why did he have to say something so stupid? A girl like Skye would never be interested in a guy like him. "I mean, I *do* take you seriously," he tried to clarify. "As a... as a friend... I..."

"You're sweet, Aaron," Skye said, smiling for the first time since Jacob's gruesome end. "It was so brave of you to come after me like that. To stand between me and that thing. I don't know how I could ever thank you. I..."

And then everything changed. The look in Skye's eyes, the one of total ignorance regarding Aaron's true feelings for her, disappeared. It was replaced by a warmth, a warmth which only grew as their eye contact lingered. Then she leaned in, licking her lips in a way that only a woman wanting a kiss does, and a thousand thoughts raced through Aaron's mind.

Was this really happening? It couldn't be. The real reason, the untold truth about why Aaron had suddenly become so reluctant to come on this Canadian road trip, was not the bullying he had suffered at the hands of Jacob at all... but his feelings for Skye. Seeing her and her muscular boyfriend together - every kiss, every touch, every erotic joke he was forced to endure - was just a harsh reminder of what he would never have.

But here they were, in a tent, entirely alone... and *she* was moving in to kiss *him*. Had she always felt something for him secretly, deep down inside? Or was this just her way of coping, her manner of finding comfort after her recent loss? Did it even matter? Not to Aaron. For once the nerd was going to get the girl, and he wasn't going to waste this golden opportunity, an opportunity that might never come again.

Pursing his lips, Aaron reciprocated, ignoring the pain in his chest as he began to sit up, his heart pounding, his palms sweating, his breath catching in his throat...

And then he saw the shadow outside of the tent.

Aaron tried to warn Skye, but his throat felt like sandpaper and all that came out was a dry wheeze. Skye leaned back, confused and completely unaware of the shape moving over them, only looking up when the roof of the tent was savagely ripped open. Her eyes widened when she finally realised the peril that she was in, but she wasn't even afforded enough time to cry for help. That chance had passed.

Claws entered the tent through the rips. Seizing Skye, they squeezed with beastly strength, crushing the bones just below her shoulders and contorting her arms into hideously unnatural positions. Pulling upwards, the claws freed her torso of her now-mangled upper limbs, and fountains of blood began to spray from the fleshy, freshly torn holes. A shower of red came down on Aaron as he watched Skye flail around like a fish that had

78

been cruelly removed from its bowl, the blood soaking every inch of the tent. Skye's eyes looked from left to right in horror, her mind desperately trying to comprehend the missing parts of her body. Then a claw came down again, the long nails passing through bone and brain, crushing the top of her skull and ending her misery. The life left Skye's eyes and, as the claw withdrew from her cranium, gripping a fistful of mushy brain, she flopped down on top of Aaron.

Now, with the once-blonde head laying on his lap, brutally punctured and mostly hollow, Aaron was grateful for his lack of glasses. Through blurred eyes he was spared the detail, and all he could make out was the surrounding veil of red. Red on the walls of the tent, red on his sleeping bag, red leaking into his eyes and mouth, a red taste, red everywhere, red, red, red...

The silhouette of the goblin appeared once again over the rear of the tent.

Finally, Aaron screamed.

TWELVE

Peter wasn't sure what was more terrifying... the sound of the bloodcurdling cry that came from his tent, or the repulsive sight he was subjected to when he whirled around, tearing his eyes away from the forest. He turned just in time to see his tent torn clean in two, exposing Aaron to the open campsite as he trembled within his sleeping bag. He was soaked in blood, Skye's armless corpse sprawled over his lap with an opened and emptied skull. And, over them both, its teeth glistening and its body dripping slime...

The goblin!

"It's back!" Lauren shrieked, her grip on Peter's arm tightening tenfold.

Seizing a manically screaming Aaron from the ruins of the tent and gripping him with both claws, the lanky, oozing goblin stared straight at Peter and Lauren, then hissed. Frozen in fright, it was only when Duke came racing back from the woodlands and through the campsite that the fearful pair followed suit, heading towards the gory scene. Bellowing another deafening screech, the goblin turned and ran, still holding Aaron with its razor-sharp nails.

Coming to a standstill in the remains of the blood-splattered tent, Skye's mauled body on the ground before them, Peter and Lauren held their mouths in unison and struggled to hold back the contents of their stomachs.

"Oh God, Skye..." Lauren said, tears welling up in her eyes.

"It's got Aaron!" Peter cried, tearing his sights away from the dismembered corpse that had once been the beautiful Skye Peterson. He looked up to see Duke pointing his rifle into the forest, tense but not pulling the trigger. "Why aren't you shooting?!"

Duke flashed Peter a glare that was more annoyed than anything else. "You ever tried aiming in the dark with one eye after three days without sleep? I need the bullets."

Peter gawked. "That thing just took off with my best friend, and you're worried about your number of *bullets?!*"

"If you wanna question my methods, kid, why don't you take this gun and see how well you-"

Screeeeeeeeee!

A demonic screech came from the darkness, but this time it wasn't one of hunger or hatred. It was one of pain.

"What was that?" Lauren gasped. "It sounded hurt!"

"That's what I'm countin' on," Duke retorted. "One of you grab the fuel. Let's see if we can smoke this fucker once n' for all!"

Aaron struggled in his sleeping bag as the goblin kept him locked within its grasp. A beartrap was clamped around its bony, scaly ankle, and the stinking green blood that seeped out only added to the grotesque stench that was coming from the creature's gooey body. Aaron hoped that the sharp steel digging into his captor's flesh and bone might be enough of a distraction for it to release him, but its grip only tightened.

"Help me!" he called desperately and, when he saw his companions appearing from the campsite nearby, he thought his prayers had been answered. Then he saw Duke drop his rifle and light a match, and his fear amplified as he realised that he was trapped between death by goblin or fiery inferno.

"Throw the damn fuel on it!" Duke ordered Peter, but Peter only took a step back.

"It's still got Aaron!" Peter said defiantly, backing away with the plastic cannister, shocked that the Canadian hunter would even suggest such a barbaric thing.

"Your friend is as good as dead!" Duke challenged him. "Throw the fuckin' fuel on it, before it-"

The goblin hissed and, with a vicious *scrunch*, it tore its leg out of the beartrap, the metal pulling away a significant chunk of flesh and bone. It cried an inhuman cry of pain but, freed from the trap, it turned and ran. Even with its mangled ankle, it was far faster than any one of the group could hope to be.

Whatever hopes Aaron had of rescue vanished as he was carried away, deeper and deeper into the midnight forest. Peter and Lauren called after him, but soon all he could hear was the savage grunting and snarling of the goblin. He feared it may be the last sound he would ever hear.

"You let it get away..." Duke bent over to pick up his rifle, and his disappointment turned to fury. "You let the fuckin' thing get away, you dumb-"

Peter's fist crashed into Duke's jaw, and the hunter dropped to the ground like a sack of flour. Before he knew what had happened, the rifle was wrenched free from his hands and Peter was standing over him, pointing his own weapon at his face.

"You wanted me to *burn my best friend alive?*"

"What that goblin has in store for him ain't much better," Duke grumbled, spitting out a glob of blood.

"And that's because of you," Peter snapped. He was genuinely contemplating squeezing the trigger. "You brought that thing here. Aaron is gone because of you. Skye is *dead* because of you!"

"You wanna blame that on me?" Duke spat. "Go right ahead. I was just doin' what had to be done."

"You could've shot it," Lauren interjected.

"I could've," Duke agreed. "But guess what, sweetheart? I already tried that, like I told you not ten damn minutes ago. Didn't stop the fucker from tearing half my face off. A bullet ain't certain. Some fuel and a match sure as shit is. That was probably the best chance we're even gonna get, and pretty boy here wasted it." Duke stood up and brushed himself off. "Now are you gonna shoot me, or can I have my goddamn gun back you lil shitwipe?"

Peter hesitated. Then, accepting that turning on each other would get them nowhere, he huffed and handed the rifle over. "So what's the plan now, Bear Grylls?"

"Don't get smart with me, kid," Duke shot back. "It's you lot that got in my way out here, not the other way 'round. I gotta hand it to you though... that's one mean right hook you got there."

"He asked you a question," Lauren snapped. "What comes next?"

Duke turned from the pair, crouched on the ground, and looked at the green blood trailing from the bear trap. Reaching down to his waist, he unsheathed a serrated hunting knife which neither Peter nor Lauren had seen until the moment the blade was out in the open. Dipping the knife into the open jaws of steel, Duke lifted up a piece of dripping flesh and scrutinised it. "Slimy sonuvabitch ripped through my beartrap like it was paper, but at least it left a trail. It'll probably keep on bleedin' throughout the night... which'll make it that much easier to track."

For a moment, Lauren almost laughed. Then she realised that Duke was being deadly serious. "Wait... are you actually suggesting we *follow* it?"

"I ain't suggestin' you do shit," Duke replied. "I'm goin' after it. You two can do whatever you want."

"We're going in the opposite direction," Lauren said without hesitation, grabbing Peter's hand and trying to lead him back to the campfire. Peter, however, didn't move an inch. He nodded at Duke, and swallowed before speaking.

"I'm not. I'm going too."

"What?" Lauren spluttered. "Peter... Peter, you can't be serious!"

"Aaron only came to Canada because I convinced him to," Peter said defiantly, looking down with guilt in his eyes. "He almost dropped out of this trip, and I'm the one who talked him back into it. I may have dragged him out here, but I'm not leaving him here too."

"But... it's suicide!" Lauren pleaded, trying to make him see reason, but it was no use.

"I don't care," Peter said firmly. "Aaron would come after me. I'm doing the same for him."

Duke shrugged. "If you ask me, your buddy's already long gone. But if you insist on comin', a second pair of hands might be useful."

Lauren looked from her friend to the hunter, exasperated. "Well it looks like I'll have to fucking come too then, doesn't it? Because I'm sure as hell not going anywhere else by myself."

"So what now?" Peter asked.

"We head back to my truck for more supplies," Duke began, "and we get everythin' we need to take that thing out... or die tryin'."

"Do you think you can track it?" Peter queried, his sights going back to the bloodied beartrap.

"Yeah," Duke confirmed casually, his tone indicating that it would be no more than a walk in the park. "But to be honest, now that I think about it, I'm not sure I'll need to... I know where it's headed. What do all animals do when they're wounded?"

Peter and Lauren shrugged in unison. Duke rolled his one eye, showing his clear disappointment in the younger generation once more. Then his expression turned into a glare, a glare which he diverted back towards the direction in which the goblin had fled.

"They go back to their nest, or wherever the hell it is they came from. We're gonna pay this thing a visit right at its goddamn doorstep."

THIRTEEN

Aaron felt himself fading as he was dragged through the black forest, the goblin clinging to his leg through the fabric of the sleeping bag. The commotion had torn the wounds in his chest open once again, and the bleeding had resumed, weakening him with every second that passed. He was not fortunate enough to be granted the gift of unconsciousness, however, and he remained perfectly aware of the nightmare he was experiencing.

His head hit a rock and he let out a slight whimper, prompting the goblin to turn and glare at him, its hideous features contorting into a snarl that he couldn't entirely see through his blurred vision. Falling into a petrified silence, Aaron tried to make his racing mind go blank. It was better than thinking about what his fate may be before the night was through.

Even with the goblin's long, gangly strides, it must have been at least an hour before they reached their destination. Aaron only discovered that they were close to whatever place the moist demon called home when the ground changed, becoming a steep slope instead of the bumpy forest floor. After being dragged down the wooded hillside, Aaron was startled by the awful sensation of cold, thick water seeping into his sleeping bag, and he didn't need his glasses to know he was in some kind of murky, watery bog. Fog swirled around and above him, and he was pulled through the wet, filthy swamp, hardly able to see through the thick mist that encased his bleeding body.

Occasionally something sharp would dig into his back or his arms. It was only when he turned his head to the side and found himself face to face with a human skull, maggots crawling out of its empty sockets as he passed by, that he felt a whole new kind of horror surge through him at the realisation of what the sharp objects were. He didn't doubt that, soon enough, his own skull would be added to the masses of bones littering the swamp, though he tried not to think such things. His natural human instinct for survival hadn't abandoned him yet, and he still feebly tried to cling to some hope that he may make it out the Canadian wilderness alive, lest his mind be lost with the acceptance of his impending doom.

The mist began to disappear, and Aaron saw a darkness overcome him. Emerging from the shallow water, he could just about make out that he was in a small cave of sorts, with a smell hanging in the air so horrendous that he almost choked on the putrid fumes. He was in the goblin's lair.

The claw gripping him by the leg let go, and Aaron closed his eyes. *This is it,* he thought suddenly. *Oh God, please, just do it quickly, please, oh God please, please...*

But death didn't come. Opening his eyes again, Aaron lifted

his head to see the vile silhouette of his captor crouching in the corner of the small cave. A sickening *crunching* and *schlurping* echoed around them both as it feasted on the remains of another, older kill.

Acknowledging that this was likely his last chance of escape, Aaron's hopes for survival returned in full force. Slowly and carefully, he leaned upwards, ignoring the sharp pain glaring across his chest as he did so. He began to unzip the sleeping bag, every muscle in his body tightening as he prayed that the goblin wouldn't hear his movements, that its noisy devouring of dead meat would be enough to mask the sounds of his gradual departure. Sliding out of the sleeping bag, Aaron began to crawl, pulling himself along the mossy floor of the small cave and out of the entrance. He soon found himself back in the mucky water, but the sensation was far less cringe-inducing knowing that the swamp was all that lay between himself and freedom.

As his creeping body descended into the low-hanging layer of fog, Aaron noticed that he was smiling. It was no normal smile, either. He had to physically repress laughter, laughter at the thought of not actually meeting his end in such a cold, desolate place after all. Every time he weakly edged himself a little further from the cave and closer to the slope leading back up to the forest, his optimism grew. And, though his thoughts of total escape were premature, it was impossible to not let his mind start believing that he would live to tell the tale of yet another encounter with this wretched being.

His smile froze when the long, slim shadow loomed over him, and then he *did* begin to laugh. There was something humorous, hysterical even, about the way he had been foolish enough to actually convince himself that he could crawl to freedom from the very domain of the ultimate predator. His insane laughter continued, the sound of it filling the swamp as he descended into utter madness, right up until the moment the four-inch claws sank into either side of his neck and pulled.

Riiiiiiip.

All pain disappeared. Aaron felt himself rise, though the weight of his body seemed to have vanished entirely. Then, as the goblin carried his still-seeing, still-conscious head back towards the cave, the last thing he witnessed was his own decapitated corpse pumping blood freely from its open neck, draining rapidly into the swamp.

FOURTEEN

It was a half an hour walk to Duke's rusty old pick-up truck for the remaining fuel cannisters, and the walk to their destination was proving much longer. Another hour passed by, and after a few miles both Peter and Lauren were beginning to struggle, needing to stop every ten minutes to catch their breath. They were lugging two plastic cannisters each, one in each hand, and they weren't nearly as accustomed to such physical labour as a natural survivor like Duke was. After their fourth pause for rest, the hunter began to grow impatient.

"It's alright, kids," he grumbled. "Not like we got anywhere important t'be."

"Just give us a minute," Peter snapped back, dropping the cannisters and leaning against the body of a pine tree. "It's my best friend out there, remember? I'm going as fast as I can."

Duke huffed, dropped the cannister he was carrying along with his rifle, and sparked up a cigarette as he waited. Somehow, even a smoker's lungs did little to affect his stamina.

"How is *he* not out of breath yet?" Peter asked Lauren, bewildered as he stared at the forty-eight year old who was seemingly more resilient to the elements that he was.

"He does have a son to avenge..." Lauren pointed out.

"Oh, yeah..." Peter sighed, suddenly feeling a twang of shame for the punch he had thrown into Duke's jaw, even if it wasn't entirely uncalled for given the circumstances. "I keep forgetting about that."

"We do a lot for the people we care about." Lauren put a hand on Peter's shoulder. "You're a good guy, Peter. Aaron is lucky to have you as a friend."

"If you say so," Peter replied, unconvinced. "Like I said, he only came out here because of me. I just hope he's still... still..."

"I'm sure he's okay," Lauren said reassuringly, trying to believe the words herself. They exchanged a weak smile, completely unaware that their friend was far beyond saving by now.

Looking at Lauren - her brunette hair, her big brown eyes - Peter realised that this might be his final chance to tell her his true feelings. He tried to think of the right words, the best way to tell her after so much horror, but nothing came to mind. Instead, he opted to just tell her the simple truth. What did he have to lose?

"Lauren..."

"You kids ready yet?" Duke called over impatiently, flicking his cigarette butt into the shadows and picking his rifle and gas cannister back up. "Let's get a move on. I might be a tough ol' bastard, but I want this t'be my last night without any goddamn sleep. Hell, even dyin' would be a welcome rest right about now."

92

Duke carried on, delving deeper and deeper into the forest, leaving Peter and Lauren to pick up their own cannisters and hurry after him.

"What were you going to say?" Lauren asked curiously.

"Nothing," Peter replied. The moment of courage had passed. He was using enough of it just to keep himself moving forwards.

Close to another hour passed, and by then even Duke was panting heavily. He leaned over and began coughing, spitting a glob of phlegm into the dirt. Peter and Lauren came to a standstill behind him, each of them breathing so heavily that their lungs threatened to burst every time they inhaled, and Peter almost fell to his knees. "Damn it... Duke... how much longer... do we... have to walk?"

"Yeah..." Lauren wheezed. "Where the... the fuck... are we even going... anyway? How far away... is this nest... or whatever it is?"

Duke wiped his mouth with his camo jacket sleeve and stared straight ahead. "See for yourselves."

Looking onwards, Peter and Lauren noticed that they had reached a change of scenery. Ahead of them the ground dropped down, and what lay at the bottom of the woodland hill was a landscape straight from the depths of hell.

A murky, foggy swamp stretched out beyond the trio, with small mounds of earth sticking out of the mist that hung a foot or two above the wet earth. In the centre stood a small hill, a cave opening on the side of it facing them like a hungry mouth, willing them to enter and be swallowed whole by the abyss. And, though it was dark and there was little light to illuminate the scene, none of the three standing before the swamp needed to be able to see any clearer to know that this was a place of death and evil.

"This ain't my first time here," Duke growled. "But it sure as shit better be my fuckin' last." Then, without hesitation, he began trudging down the steep, slippery slope.

"Is it too late to turn back?" Peter croaked, a strange noise coming from his throat that sounded like a forced laugh. He and Lauren looked back, the notion of fleeing for the road, never to return, crossing their minds briefly. Instead they gulped and turned to face the swamp, following Duke and making their way into the vast, putrid pit of despair.

Reaching the bottom of the slope, lugging their cannisters and struggling to keep their footing, the swamp offered little relief. It may not have been quite so difficult to walk across, but cold, filthy water began seeping through Peter and Lauren's boots, causing both of them to grimace in disgust. Then came the cracking of animal bones from beneath their feet, bones hidden by the swirling fog, and their disgust turned to pure dread.

Holding her breath, Lauren moved a step closer to Peter. The hill cave lay only a few feet ahead now, and its interior came into clear view.

The roof of the cave inside the hill, a partially hollow mound only about twice as tall as Duke, was hanging with roots and dripping with muddy water, the droplets falling to a floor covered in moss and fungi. And, in a pile in the centre of the cave floor, lay a mass of bones - mostly animal, but some human too.

Lauren gasped and took a step back. "What *is* this place?"

"Somewhere we don't wanna spend any more time than we need to," Duke grunted. Still holding his rifle in one hand, he opened the cannister he was gripping in the other with his teeth and splashed some of the fuel onto the bones. "The slimy bastard ain't here now, thank fuck, but it'll be back. Lace the cave with fuel, but don't use it all. Put the cannisters down around the bones when you're done too. When the damn thing returns, I'm gunna pop a bullet into one of the containers here from afar and blow the slimy shit into orbit."

Peter and Lauren did as they were told, splashing the fuel around the cave before placing the partially emptied cannisters in a small circle around the pile of bones. Soon their trap was set, and Duke allowed himself a satisfied smirk.

"You sure this'll work?" Peter asked.

"If this don't, nothin' will," Duke replied. "Just need to get outta here now, and wait for that thing to come home."

Peter and Duke were so busy looking at the fuel-soaked remains of the goblin's victims that neither of them had been paying attention to the swamp outside of the cave. Lauren, however, was looking back in the direction they had come from, and what she saw made her heart jump into her throat. Stepping back, she grabbed Peter's hand. "I don't think we're going to need to wait for that."

Screeeeeeee!

Peter and Duke span around hastily and, sure enough, in the distance atop the slope leading into the swamp stood the goblin. In its long, slender arm it held something, and before any of the group could wonder what it was, the goblin threw it across the swamp towards them with unnatural strength. Soaring through the air, the object landed inside the cave and rolled up to the side of the stripped bones.

It was Aaron's head, the flesh around his neck hanging messily in strips of red and pink.

"Aaron..." Peter whispered. The shock of seeing the remains of his friend, the sole reason he had ventured into this hateful lair, rendered him speechless. Lauren choked back tears at the sight, burying her face into Peter's chest, unable to stand the disturbing sight of terror lingering on Aaron's dead face. Duke, his expression remaining hard and cold, lifted his eyes from the severed head, and his disgusted gaze fell on the goblin.

It was time to get even.

"You two get yourselves outta here," Duke said, his grip tightening around his rifle as the goblin began crawling down the slope on all fours, its limbs contorting and twisting in the most hideous fashion as it reached the swamp. "Me and this fucker have some unfinished business."

"I'm not leaving you," Peter said firmly, his shock turning to pure hatred. "I'm helping you kill this thing."

"No you ain't," Duke shot back. "I've got one gun, and even that might not be enough. If I can't take it down, you sure as hell can't. Take the girl and get as far away as you can. This sonuvabitch has killed enough people."

Peter stood his ground reluctantly, but Lauren grabbed him by the hand. "Peter," she pleaded. "Peter, please. We don't have to die here tonight."

Looking from Duke to Lauren, wrestling with his desire for revenge and his will to live, he eventually receded. He and Lauren stepped out of the cave and began making their way to the side of the swamp, walking around the approaching goblin which had its eyes set on Duke. This was personal.

Duke stepped out of the cave, raised his rifle, and fired.

Bang!

The first shot missed. Cursing, he raised his rifle again, and aimed the best that he could with his one eye.

Bang!

The second shot skimmed the goblin's lean, grey-green thigh, and it hissed as it continued to storm towards the cave, hunger visible in its plain white eyes.

Bang!

The third shot tore a chunk out of the goblin's bony shoulder, and it shuddered, letting out a cry of pain.

Bang!

The fourth shot missed as Duke's foot sank an inch into the moss and threw him slightly off balance. The goblin was only a few feet away. Dropping his rifle, Duke snarled, showing his own teeth in an animalistic fashion, and drew his serrated hunting knife. Wielding the eight-inch blade, its edge glimmering in the moonlight, he marched towards the goblin through the water. "Alright then, you slimy, stinkin', crawlin' piece of goblin shit. Let's do this your way."

Duke Hunter and the swamp goblin let out the most ferocious death cries they had to offer, and met outside of the hill cave in a fight to the death.

Swiping the knife, Duke caught the goblin's stomach with a shallow slash, green blood spraying through the air. He swiped again, as fast as he could, but the goblin was faster. It caught his arm and twisted, almost break his wrist. With its other claw, it ripped a chunk of flesh out of his hip, and Duke roared in agony. Before the goblin could remove any more skin, he drove his forehead into its face, headbutting it and sending its lanky frame stumbling backwards. Wiping the slime from his forehead, Duke check his hip and saw blood pumping from the wound.

"It's gonna take more than that," he laughed, deeply and menacingly, then lunged forwards again. The goblin replied in kind, throwing its crooked frame towards the hunter, and his knife sank deep into its ribcage.

Such an injury would have killed any normal animal - but this was no normal animal. Ignoring the blade sticking halfway into its torso, the goblin grabbed Duke with both of its claws and lifted him into the air. Its nails sank deep into his chest, and he let out bellow of pain, struggling to free himself from the goblin's grip. His enemy only hissed, its long ears pointing backwards in inhuman satisfaction, its wrinkled nose crumpling at the scent of fresh blood, and it opened its jaws to tear out his jugular.

Scrunch!

The goblin shrieked, its empty eyes widening as it dropped Duke into the foggy swamp and turned around. A sharp, broken bone had been driven into its back, and its long arms flailed as it tried to reach for it and pull it back out. When it turned, the goblin saw Peter standing there, his hands now empty, the bone serving as his only means of immediate attack or defence. Lauren stood a few feet behind him, her hands covering her mouth when she realised that her one remaining friend had just lost his only weapon, a weapon still embedded into the goblin's back, and she screamed.

"What are you doing?!" Duke yelled from the misty floor. "Get outta here, damn it!"

"I couldn't leave you!" Peter yelled back, but those were the only words he could get out. The goblin lunged forwards, seizing him, and clamped its teeth around his shoulder.

Peter cried out as blood poured down his green coat, the pain of the goblin's teeth sinking into his flesh and muscle excruciating. Fortunately for him, Lauren also possessed the courage to stand up to the goblin and, seizing a human skull from the swamp floor, she smashed it into the creature's face.

The goblin released Peter and stumbled backwards, its gangly arms raising defensively in front of its face. Peter fell to the floor and Lauren raced to his side to check that he was okay. He wasn't, but he was alive, and fortunately the bite wasn't deep enough to be fatal.

The goblin recovered swiftly from the blow. It stood over the pair and opened its jaws, hissing, its breath foul enough to choke on even from a few feet away. It took a step forwards, preparing to finish both of them off before they could intervene any further, but it was stopped dead in its tracks.

Leaping forwards, covered in wounds but still alive, Duke grabbed hold of the hilt of his hunting knife where it was still planted between the goblin's ribs and twisted. The goblin span back to face him, screeching, and grabbed him where he knelt on the swamp floor by his throat. Lifting him upwards again, higher and higher until his feet were no longer touching the floor, it began carrying the hunter back to the cave to finish him off.

"Go!" Duke spluttered, barely able to get the words out. "Go, now!"

Lauren helped Peter to his feet, and they began to retreat from the swamp, making for the slope. They reached the bottom as the goblin entered its cave with Duke, both of them feeling a great deal of guilt for leaving the hunter behind, but also accepting that there was nothing more they could do. Climbing the slope, they both knew that their only hopes of survival were in fleeing.

Inside the cave, Duke's face began to turn purple as the life was choked out of him. Standing in the pile of bones, the goblin held him high as he looked around frantically, searching for anything that might help him survive. As his lungs began to fail, his throat desperately trying to suck in the foul air as the goblin's claws dug into his neck, one image lingered in his mind before his body gave up entirely.

The image of his son.

The goblin showed its teeth. Duke looked down and saw the red plastic in the dark. The jaws of death came towards his face and, when they were only inches away, he laughed a breathless laugh. The goblin tilted its head, confused by the laughter, only realising the cause when it was too late.

Having pulled a match from his camo jacket pocket, Duke raised his hand and struck the head with his thumb nail. The flame flickered and came to life.

The goblin's grip loosened ever-so-slightly, its eyes showing genuine fear for the first time in its cursed life, and Duke Hunter's laughter died. In the moment before he dropped the match into the fuel-soaked bones surrounded by plastic flammable cannisters, he managed to speak one final time. His husky, exhausted wheezing was laced with a tone of vengeful triumph.

"Feast on this, you ugly mother-"

Screeeeeeeeeee!

FIFTEEN

Peter and Lauren reached the top of the slope as the explosion lit up the swamp behind them. Even from afar, they could feel the heat of the flames as the hill in which the goblin's lair resided became engulfed with fire, a shockwave rippling through the low blanket of fog. The blast was deafening, and they both turned around to witness the inferno as it obliterated the hill-cave and surrounding swamplands.

When the smoke began to clear, all that was left were clumps of flaming debris sinking into the rancid sludge, the lair mostly decimated. There were no signs of Duke nor the creature, but nothing could have survived such a catastrophic event.

It was over. The goblin was no more.

"Duke..." Peter gasped, clutching his bleeding shoulder, red leaking between his fingers.

"Come on," Lauren said, turning back to the forest ahead and pulling Peter with her. "We have to get out of here."

Neither of them felt any joy at the death of the creature responsible for turning their travels into a traumatizing and near-unbelievable bloodbath. Relief, perhaps, that they were no longer in any danger, but the cost had been dear. They trekked away from the swamp, exhausted and silent, both of them solemnly reflecting on their dead friends and the nightmare they had endured.

Soon dawn began to break, making the Canadian forest a little easier to travel in the dim, orange glow of the rising sun. Heading in the direction they believed their camp lay, luck was finally on their side. It took some time with the slow pace they were forced to travel at due to Peter's injury, but they stumbled across their tents as dawn became morning.

Trying to ignore the horrible sight of Skye's mangled body, as well as the shredded and blood-splattered tent, Peter reluctantly retrieved the keys for the minivan from his nearby rucksack. They left everything else they had brought with them behind. They had their lives, and that was all they cared to keep as long as it meant getting out of the wilderness as soon as possible.

Many more miles lay between their ruined campsite and their minivan, but finding Badger's Trail was no longer an issue with daylight above them. But, when they finally emerged onto the section of the trail that they and their now-deceased companions had so recently stood upon, debating which way to go to find a decent camping spot, Peter stopped and turned around. His eyes lingered back in the direction of the carnage, and he hung his head.

"We'll come back for them," Lauren reassured him. "I promise."

"I can't believe this..." Peter croaked. "Any of it... Aaron...

Jacob... Skye... this shouldn't have happened... this shouldn't-"

Suddenly, as if out of nowhere, his speech was interrupted by Lauren's lips pressing against his, ending his words of mourning. At first he was taken aback entirely but, when he realised what was happening, he kissed back - hesitantly to begin with, but then with more passion.

When they finally released each other, Peter stared into Lauren's eyes and a weak smile broke onto his face. "You have no idea how long I've wanted that."

Lauren forced a smile back. "I do now." She clasped his face with her hands. "There's nothing more we could have done, Peter... but *we* made it at least. Now let's get the fuck out of here and never go into the woods again."

A few more hours passed, but by midday they had reached the end of Badger's Trail to find their minivan waiting exactly where they had left it the day before. Pulling out the keys, Peter unlocked the van and opened the driver's side door. He tried to climb into the seat behind the wheel, but Lauren was having none of it.

"You must think I'm mad if you think I'm going to let you drive us back to the city looking like that," she said, nodding at his ravaged shoulder. "I didn't live through the night we've just had for you to drive us off a cliff."

Laughing weakly, Peter handed her the keys. She had a point.

Moments later they were on the road, the greenery passing them by in a blur of green and brown. Peter opened the window to feel the wind on his face but, despite the cold, the toll of all he had been through was too great to enjoy the sensation. He fought to keep his eyes open, but it was no use. Soon he was drifting off as Lauren drove them further and further from the nightmare that had finally come to an end.

The last thought that crossed his mind before he fell into a deep, dreamless sleep in the passenger's seat was of Duke. He felt sorry that the grizzled Canadian hunter had had to die alongside the wretched being responsible for killing his son, but perhaps it was for the better. With seemingly nothing left to live for, a hard man like Duke Hunter could ask for little more than vengeance fulfilled in a final blaze of glory.

Then sleep came to Peter, and the pain in his shoulder faded with the gentle humming of the minivan.

SIXTEEN

The flames had long died by the time darkness began to fall over the swamp once again. The natural sounds of the forest were returning, now that the goblin was gone and the creatures of the British Columbian woodlands were free of the terror it had brought. Where it had come from, none of those who had faced it the previous night could say, but it was gone now and that was all that mattered.

The swamp was still beneath the swirling mist and, though its vile stench lingered, no human nose remained to inhale the unfathomable stench. None, save one.

"Son of a bitch..." Duke groaned, wincing in agony as he pushed the chunks of earth, root, and bone away, painfully climbing out of the remains of the small cave. He was battered and bleeding, burnt and bruised, caked in filth and blood... but the hardened Canadian hunter was a survivor, and survive he would.

Rising on shaking legs, he forced himself to walk on, fighting death with every breath that escaped his lungs. Stepping upon crunchy bone, the thick, sloppy water lapping at his boots, he looked like a ghost wandering through the fog, the one eye that remained on his red and blistered face fixed on the slope ahead.

"I'd give my left nut for a smoke right now," he grumbled, not entirely convinced that his left nut actually still remained to him at all. It was a miracle that he hadn't been blown to pieces in the blast. His burns were bad, his camouflage garments incinerated in many places, and his countless wounds niggled every time he moved. The layer of filth would be sure to riddle him with infection if he didn't get to a hospital soon, but his truck was near and he was sure that he could drive at the very least.

Reaching the base of the slope, he slowly began to climb. If he was lucky, he could make it to the truck before total darkness covered the woodlands. And, considering all he had been through over the last few days, a bit of luck didn't seem like too much to ask for.

He didn't look back. He didn't want to think about the creature he had battled, the ordeal he had survived... the death of his son.

"Sam..." he sighed, then pressed on. There would be time to mourn later. Until then, there was a little way yet to go, and at least he could be satisfied in knowing that the abomination responsible for taking what meant most to him in the world had paid with its life.

Reaching the top of the slope in slow, laborious strides, Duke never saw the slimy claw rising from the mist behind him.

FEAST

OF THE

SWAMP GOBLIN

FOR MORE BY THE AUTHOR, VISIT...

FACEBOOK.COM/LEWISSTONEOFFICIAL

INSTAGRAM.COM/LEWISSTONEAUTHOR

Printed in Great Britain
by Amazon

50039506R00064